I0772819

ALL THE FEELS

Volume 1: A Collection of Six Inspiring Short Stories

B. A. PAUL

Contents

Foreword   v

The Snowglobe Effect   1
I, Mae Dae   13
The Sunrise Project   23
Replacing Carrots   34
The Gatherer   49
All the Knitted Unicorns   58

About the Author   71
Also by B. A. Paul   73

Copyright © 2020 by B.A. Paul

This collection and the works therein are licensed for your personal enjoyment only. All rights reserved. This is a work of fiction. All characters and events portrayed herein are fictional, and any resemblance to real people or incidents is purely coincidental. This work, or parts thereof, may not be reproduced in any form without permission.

"The Snowglobe Effect" © 2017 and first printed in Twenty-One Short Stories: Momentary Escapes from the Mundane by B. A. Paul. "The Gatherer" © 2017 and first printed in Twenty-One Short Stories: Momentary Escapes from the Mundane by B. A. Paul. "The Sunrise Project" © 2017 and first printed in Twenty-One Short Stories: Momentary Escapes from the Mundane by B. A. Paul. "I, Mae Dae" © 2019 by B.A. Paul; "Replacing Carrots" © 2019 by B.A. Paul; "All the Knitted Unicorns" © 2020 by B.A. Paul.

Foreword

I'm not a romance writer, not by a very long stretch of the imagination, but sometimes the stories that pour from my fingertips hint at the beginnings of something special.

A possibility.

A spark.

That brush of human connection that we all long for, even if we're not actively seeking Mr. or Mrs. Right.

The tales in *All the Feels: Volume 1* are not quite romances, but they all have that possibility. What happens after the last line, well, I left that up to the characters to find their own ways. I simply pointed them toward a certain kind of horizon.

It's also up to you, dear reader, to imagine what may happen next. To paint your own happily-ever-after scenario and maybe scratch your feeler right where it itches.

Happy reading!

B. A. Paul

The Snowglobe Effect

When her daughter's most treasured possession is ruined, single mother and war widow Maranda must scramble to have it mended… and in the process, she might find more mending than she ever could have hoped for.

*T*he shrill shrieks and panicked footsteps from her daughter's bedroom early Saturday morning caused Maranda's heart to skip a beat. She dropped the skillet into the dishwater. Liz stood behind her already, tears streaking her flushed face.

"I need water. I need water. They're all gonna die."

Maranda relaxed a bit when she realized this chaos was about the fish. She reached for the large red mixing bowl and filled it with tepid water. "I'll carry it for you."

Liz shook her head. "I can do it. Just hurry."

This would be the third time this month that Liz or Jonas knocked over the goldfish bowl in Liz's room. Maranda would have to move the fish to the kitchen counter for everyone's sanity.

"Be careful!" Liz walked stiff-armed, the bowl sloshing water over its sides all down the hallway. Maranda had mopped the day before.

She searched under the sink for the goldfish net and treatment kit. Poor things probably wouldn't survive this time. There were two left out of the three the kids had won at the fair last summer. Maranda didn't think fair fish were supposed to survive the car ride home, but here they were, still feeding and caring for them.

Three more mouths, albeit small ones, on her meager bank teller's salary.

She didn't want to deal with two fish bowls, so the kids took turns taking care of them. One month on. One month off. The first time the bowl spilled, Jonas had been trying to steal it back to his room and had tripped in the hallway, so he'd lost a month of fish privileges.

Maranda filled a pitcher with water, added the treatment drops and carried it to Liz's room.

Liz sat on the floor, back to the door, transferring her beloveds to the red mixing bowl from the carpet, talking softly to each one.

But the goldfish bowl sat on the dresser and the three fish swam peacefully in circles.

"Liz, whatcha got there?"

"They were gonna die, Mommy. I couldn't let them die."

Maranda knelt beside her daughter on the wet carpet. Glitter and glass and tiny figurines had scattered all over the floor. Liz picked through the glass to find each caroler dressed in reds and greens, the Big Ben clock tower and the tiny puppy and kitten that had been part of the mural under the dome.

Her small fingers bled tinges of pink onto the cream carpet and stained her jeans as she wiped them on her knees after transferring two of the carolers into the red mixing bowl. Maranda grabbed Liz's hands, forcing her to make eye contact.

"Mommy, please, I can't find the man. The little man in the white scarf." She tried to pull away.

"Let me help you, sweetheart. You're cutting your fingers on the glass."

Liz yanked away hard. "I don't care. He's suffocating. I have to find him."

"Liz! I said let me help." Maranda couldn't care less about the snow globe inhabitants. She only wanted to prevent Liz from doing further damage to herself. She scanned the carpet, but didn't see the figure. The base of the globe had landed next to the fish, tipped on its side. It must've fallen from the shelf above.

She rose to inspect the dresser. The little man, caught under the weight of the base, lay in three tiny parts.

"Here he is." She held out the broken figure for Liz to see.

"No!" she wailed and grabbed the caroler from Maranda's palm, leaving drops of blood in his place.

Liz gently dropped the parts into the water, pulled her knees up to her chest and sobbed. Maranda joined her daughter on the floor and wrapped her arms around the heartbroken child. She kissed the top of her head. "We'll figure out how to fix it. We'll find a way to make it okay." She pulled Liz's face up by the chin to meet hers. "But we have to get your fingers looked at first."

"I killed him, Mommy. I killed the little man."

"No, sweetheart. It was an accident."

"Daddy said. Daddy said I should take real good care of it and now I've killed the little man." She pulled away from Maranda and sobbed into her kneecaps again.

Tom had picked up the snow globe for Liz two years ago on his way home from deployment. He gave Jonas his combat helmet. He greeted Maranda with a hand-crafted snow globe that contained a figurine of a long-stemmed white rose, much like the one she'd carried on their wedding day, though his much-awaited presence after a long stint in the desert would have been enough for her. He'd made it home in time for Christmas that year.

It was the last Christmas they'd spent together.

And then Maranda understood. The globe was the last gift Tom had given Liz. They'd spent hours tipping it this way and that, watching the glittering snow dust swirl and settle. They would make up stories and personalities for the carolers. They'd even named the dog and cat.

He'd built the shelf above her dresser for the globe and promised to bring her one each time he came back from deployment.

Maranda choked back tears and lifted the protesting Liz from the carpet. "We have to take you to the clinic." Liz wrapped arms and legs around her tightly and nestled her head in the crook of Maranda's neck, soaking her t-shirt with tears and blood.

A muffled "What about the people?" came between tears.

"They'll be fine in the bowl until we get home. Jonas! Come quick. We're going to town!" Maranda grabbed keys, purse and her grumpy ten-year-old boy and loaded them into the CR-V.

AFTER FILLING up at the gas station, the bribery McDonald's Happy Meals, the clinic's co-pay to pick tiny shards of glass out of three little fingers and glue a laceration on Liz's palm, Maranda was nearly out of cash.

She dropped the kids off at Tom's mother's, a relationship forged with much trial and error after Tom's passing, and returned home to clean up the mess in peace. She feared Liz would sprint to her bedroom and reinjure herself checking on the people in the red bowl.

Two hours later, after she had a fan drying the carpet, the red bowl drained and refilled with glass-free water to cover the people, including the sawed-in-half man with the broken arm, and some light housekeeping, she was ready to solve the problem of the snow globe.

She searched online for a similar globe to no avail. Liz wouldn't fall for it anyway. The kid never missed a detail. She turned the base over in her hands; the dome was shattered beyond repair. With the right tools, one might be able to scrape away the remnants of the globe from the base and start from scratch. But she had no idea where to begin.

For kicks, she searched for snow globe repair, but the closest thing was a watch and grandfather clock repair shop ten miles away in the old downtown Bellview. She'd only been to that neighborhood a couple of times, to the antique shops with Tom's mother on one of their attempts at bonding.

It was worth a try. The shop was still open and she could pick up the kids on the way home. She retrieved the emergency credit card taped behind the dresser. If Tom were here, he'd say she was being silly, spending the money on such a trivial thing. But Tom wasn't here, and the globe and its history were part of him. And very much a part of Liz's memories of him.

On her way out of the bedroom, she paused to pick up the white rose globe he'd given her. Maybe the dome could be used from this one to repair Liz's. She'd keep the rose, of course, but Liz could have the parts. She wrapped the globe securely in a pillow case and retrieved the broken base and the bowl from the kitchen.

She had no idea why she kept water over the figures. At least she'd honestly be able to tell Liz that she hadn't let anyone suffocate on her watch.

MARANDA STRUGGLED to open the door to the shop with her full hands. She should've just dumped the water and put the figures in a baggie, but her mommy brain was worn thin.

The shop was dimly lit except for a magnifying lamp attached to a metal arm and hooked to the end of a long wooden work table. The lone employee acknowledged her, but did not look up, when the door chime sounded behind her. His hands were the brightest things in the room under the harsh light.

"Be with you in just a moment."

She readjusted the load in her arms and took in row upon row of clocks. Some hung on the walls, some grandfather models towered above shorter shelves with even more timepieces. One wall was devoted entirely to cuckoos. They all ticked and tocked to their own rhythm and she wondered how anyone could concentrate with the cacophony of beats.

"Okay. How may I help you?" The man stood, removed the lighted headpiece and offered her a hand. When he realized she couldn't shake hands, he helped her set down the red bowl, base and pillowcase. "Well, that's certainly not a clock." He picked up the base and turned it over in his hands.

Maranda explained what had happened and her difficulty in finding a solution. She left out the sentimental aspect, as most anyone could guess by the effort she took that the snow globe was special.

"Well, I do have some tools and an epoxy that might work. I'll be honest, though. This would be my first snow globe procedure." He smiled and met her with the kindest blue eyes she'd ever seen. She was surprised that he wasn't a gray-haired, hunchbacked old guy that had worked the shop all his life. She hadn't been expecting someone close to her age.

He offered his hand once again, and she shook it. He grinned again and said, "It looks like you really did have a rough day."

Maranda pulled back and looked down at her shirt. A hot mess of dishwater, glitter and blood. In the chaos, she'd forgotten what she must look like. She blushed and looked down to the polished concrete floor.

"Sorry, didn't mean to embarrass. I can tell it's been a long day." He turned to the table and the red bowl. Most of the water had sloshed out onto the floormats on the way to the repair shop. "I'll do what I can to help save your little girl's carolers. It may not be exactly the same, but at least they'll be back under water."

"I know it's ridiculous, but she really thought they would die if we didn't—"

"No, no. Not ridiculous at all." He fished out the broken man and held the parts in his palm. "After I've finished, I'll give you a call. And bring the kids in next time. They'd like to hear the clocks go off, I'm sure." He nodded over his shoulder toward the wall of cuckoos.

"Well, apparently they're both accident prone. I'm not sure you'd want them in your—"

"Nonsense. There's nothing broken that can't be fixed."

Maranda tried not to tear up, though she had no idea where the emotion was coming from. Probably stress and the weight of the day.

She turned to leave when the man said, "I'm Rick, by the way. It was nice to meet you." Maranda looked back and smiled, blushed again, and stumbled out the door.

ON SUNDAY, Maranda found herself checking her phone. She didn't know if it was because of Liz's constant questions about whether Mr. Rick from the clock shop could fix her globe or something else. The shop wouldn't open again until Monday. She shouldn't expect a call until tomorrow or Tuesday, and she explained as much to Liz.

She went about fixing the kids' lunches and laying out school clothes for the next day. She couldn't put her finger on what she was experiencing. She was anxious about the bill for the repair. Anxious about the bills for everything, but that kind of anxiety she was used to, and had been for quite some time.

She sliced an apple and divided it between two plates alongside the pizza rolls and called the kids to the table. What she felt was more like anticipation. Some foreign emotion that had a slight familiarity to it.

Jonas reached the table first and promptly knocked over his glass of milk. She curbed the surge of angry aggravation, grabbed a towel for the mess and refilled his glass.

No wonder she couldn't figure herself out. She'd been in survival mode for over two years.

She was clearing the dishes when the phone rang. Her hands were full, as they always seemed to be, and she couldn't get to the call before it went to voicemail. After she shoved sidewalk chalk at the kids and then shoved them out the back door, she retrieved the message.

It was Rick.

Her heart stopped. Like it used to when she and Tom were dating.

Waves of guilt washed over her and she didn't even hear the message. She sank to the kitchen floor and tried to gather herself before one of the kids walked in. After she chided herself for the apparent school girl crush, she hit replay and listened this time.

The snow globe was fixed. She could pick it up today. Sunday. If she came before three, he'd set all the cuckoos to go off at the same time for the kids to see.

She straddled indecision on whether to call him back and let him know she'd come or to simply show up. She decided to call.

No. Never mind. She'd just text the number back: Okay, be there before three.

When she hit send, her pulse quickened, another wave of guilt and shame and beads of sweat started on her forehead. Oh. My. Word. Then it occurred to her she may have texted a landline. But her phone said "sent."

The reply was quick: Great. Looking forward to meeting Miss Liz and her brother.

It was two o'clock. Time to round up the natives.

~

SHE STOPPED the kids on the sidewalk in front of the clock store. "What did I say?"

In unison they replied, "Don't touch anything."

"What else?"

"Be nice," Jonas rolled his eyes and she tapped him on the back of the head.

"Say thank you." Liz jumped on her tip toes. Maranda had barely had time to rebandage her hands before they left, the sidewalk chalk and driveway dirt had taken their toll on the wraps.

Maranda held open the door and whispered, "Don't touch anything. Not one thing."

"Woah!" Jonas was off, running his index finger over two grandfather clocks before Maranda could stop him.

"It's okay, really. Do you like those?" Rick held out his hand in greeting, Jonas shook it without taking his eyes off the biggest clock in the shop.

"I'm so sorry. I told them not to—"

"It really is okay. You can relax." His smile stirred up butterflies she hadn't felt for fifteen years.

"You must be Liz. I think I have something for you." Rick led her to the worktable where he pointed to a lump underneath a hunter green cloth. "Are you ready?"

She nodded, wide-eyed, her bandaged hands resting on the edge of the table.

Rick pulled the cloth from the globe. Maranda and Jonas bent behind her for a closer look.

"Mom! It's amazing! And look at the little man!" She couldn't take her eyes off the globe. Rick had reassembled the carolers—in a different configuration of course—but all of them were accounted for. Even the dog and the cat. Big Ben stood proudly in the distance and the little man now wore a belt around his waist and his arm hung in a sling.

"Rick, how did you even think to do this? This is amazing!"

Rick stood up tall behind the table. "I enjoyed working on something so unique and so different. It really was a blast." He turned to Liz. "I hope the little man is to your liking."

"He's just great. Just great!" She reached for the globe, but Rick stopped her.

"Here. I think this will work best for the ride home." He put the repaired snow globe into a box lined with Styrofoam and shut the lid. "Leave it on the table until 3:01, though."

Liz looked confused. "Why?"

Rick winked at her and said, "You'll see."

About then the clocks, hundreds of clocks, struck three. The cuckoo wall came alive with all manner of birds, elves, forest creatures and dancing Swiss children. Jonas and Liz were awestruck. Maranda, despite the racket, enjoyed the display as much as the children.

As the minute wound down, the clocks swallowed their inhabitants behind tiny wooden doors, and the shop returned to its unkempt rhythm.

"I have something for you too, Jonas." The boy whirled his attention from the wall to the shopkeeper, who held a plastic bag and a wooden box. Inside the bag were gears, clock hands and even a cuckoo bird. Inside the box, Rick showed him, were tiny tools, screw, and hinges.

"I got my start when I was about your age. I was allowed to play with the spare parts and see what I could come up with. Would you like to try?" Rick offered him the goodies, Jonas nodded and, without being asked, said thank you.

As she watched Rick and her children, Maranda felt a deep pang of guilt and sorrow. This brief interaction was the closest her kids had come to having a father figure in a long time. One to encourage. One to fix the broken things.

One to dream with.

She brushed away a rogue tear and faked a sneeze, a very bad fake sneeze, into the crook of her elbow.

Rick looked at her with those warm eyes and said, "Did you think I'd forget about you?" He motioned her to the table and pointed to another lump. This one under a purple cloth. "I used every part of your globe to fix hers. Except for two things." He lifted the purple cloth.

Under it, in a clear crystal vase, was the white rose.

"Mommy, see? He knows. He knows the things in the globes need water." Indeed, Rick had filled the little vase with real water, and situated the rose inside.

Maranda was speechless. She brought her hands up to her face to hide her emotion and choked out a thank you.

He boxed up the rose and Jonas's clock parts. He handed the repaired globe in its box to Liz and helped them out the door.

Once the kids were in the car, he pulled Maranda to the side-walk and handed her a pink slip of paper. "Oh, I almost forgot to pay you." She reached for her purse, but he put a hand on her arm to stop her.

"It's not a bill. There's no charge. Really. You brought me all the parts I needed, so—"

"I insist—"

"I won't take your money." Rick nodded to the paper. "I found that. In the base of your globe under the felt pad. I didn't read it, I promise. But the paper is much newer than the globe, so I thought whoever gave you the rose, must've left you a note."

She didn't try to stop the torrent of tears this time. She turned the paper over in her hand and nodded. "Thank you."

"You're welcome." He squeezed her arm and went back into the shop.

SHE HELPED Liz make room on her dresser for the snow globe to prevent a repeat episode. She relocated the fair fish to the kitchen counter in the process.

Jonas sat at the table, engrossed in gears and screws and hinges.

Maranda retreated to her bedroom, pulled the pink paper from her jeans and sat on the edge of the bed. She unfolded it slowly, the creases crisp from the weight of the water under the dome.

Tom's scrawl was unmistakable.

I'm going to the front lines. I couldn't bear to tell you, and I'm such a coward to leave a note in a place you may never find it. I love you, Maranda.

Be happy. Help the kids find joy.

And, when the time is right, find love again.

She wiped away the tears, refolded the note and placed it under the vase on her nightstand.

Maranda smiled. Perhaps the time was now.

I, Mae Dae

Life for Mae is a daily struggle. Born with a deformity and reared in the foster system, she's faced obstacles that no young girl should ever face. But Mae has what it takes to overcome.
Mae Dae has heart.

*M*rs. Price said human brains have two parts: The smart part and the heart part. And she told me 'twas okay that I didn't get much of the smart, because I got plenty of heart. I adjust the headband on my bright blue City Burger visor and look out the dust-covered window of the Blue Line bus. Blue Line to 24th Street stop. I have to pay close attention or I'll miss my get-off. Because I have more heart than smarts, Mrs. Price said to concentrate real hard on the stops and where the lit-up street names above the bus driver's head says we are.

Twenty-Second Street. That's one…two more stops. Three people get off and two get on. A little more wiggle room. A little less summer stink from all the hot bodies.

I fiddle with the ends of my ponytail. I'm glad I got my white daddy's smooth hair and not my black momma's kinky curls. Not so glad I got a daddy in jail and a momma in the ground. That's caused me all kinds of worry. I remember their hair, though. I remember playing beauty parlor on the floor of our old single-wide trailer before Daddy burnt it down. I'd run my doll's combs through their hairs and feel how different. And put makeups on Momma and sometimes Daddy when he was sleepin' off whatever he took in.

I smudge my initials on the window next to someone else's smudged initials. MD next to whoever SF is. I worry about lots with my Momma and Daddy and all the what-nexts. Mrs. Price has been so nice and helpful and kind since I was eight years old. And she helped me get this job. And I'm an adult in a few weeks. I need to keep this job at City Burger for as long as I can. I'm one of the longest employees they got at this location.

Me and Eddie Morris.

And Miss Manda say that's 'cause me and Eddie Morris keep our heads down and do as we told with no lip.

And we don't ask off much. Nothin' much to ask off for.

Being more heart than smart, I see things other people miss, I think. Like how to treat people kind and not get all better than them. I don't ask them nothing that ain't my business when I give them their burgers or shakes or clean up their table messes. I try to smile. And Mrs. Price say if I make eye contact and smile and hold my shoulders high that them burger customers respect me more that way and be kind back.

Mostly that be true. Sometimes it ain't, though.

Twenty-Third Street now. I tap my foot and my knee jumps up and down. I gotta pay attention in a few moments when 24th street comes 'round. I gotta get situated so my left arm don't give me no grief getting down off the bus. Gimp arm. All wavy and scrawny from the elbow on down.

I rub it. It gets sore sometimes down deep in the muscles. But Mrs. Price and Miss Manda say they proud of my hard work anyhow. I don't complain about my lazy left arm. There's no use in complain' when there's stuff to be done.

I asked Mrs. Price long time back about why I am the way I am. If it was because I'm two colors wrapped in one skin. She wrapped her big white arms around me and kissed my head. And she explained that when Daddy and Momma made me that they wasn't using their smarts. Had nothin' to do with their colors. Had to do with the fact that drunk sperm don't swim straight and that's why my arm is the way it is. And that mommas on drugs and all that nastiness take away their babies' smarts sometimes.

But ain't nothin' can touch the heart part of a person if we don't let it. And my heart is good 'cause I didn't let my Momma and Daddy's deeds touch it.

I like Mrs. Price's big fat arms. Best arms ever.

The letters lit up with 24th Street. I stand up off the sticky bus seat. Sticky with heat and who knows who else's sweat. I walk a little sideways down the aisle to not bump into other people hangin' their bodies off their seats. I don't like bumpin' into no sweaty bodies right before I gotta go to work all clean and everything.

I don't much like smelling sweat or bumpin' into sweaty bodies when I *don't* gotta be at work. I take the rail real careful in my right hand and step off the bus. City Burger's lot is just ahead and my heart beats a little fast. I hope to all the good lords that that old green pickup ain't in the parking lot today. That green truck give me nightmares.

I look at my digital watch with the lit-up numbers Mrs. Price got for me for Christmas the winter before I got my City Burger job. She worked with me and the school aide worked with me until I got real good at tellin' time. I can get things like that, but takes lots of patience. And I gotta practice lots to get real good at anything smart-related.

I got ten minutes before my shift starts. That's good enough time to use the bathroom and get my Mae nametag.

And I'm so grateful Miss Manda took over after my first boss, Mr. Max, got caught takin' what wasn't his from the safe. He was always takin' what wasn't his and he finally got himself good and caught. And he'd always made fun of my name.

I'd go home crying from City Burger several times a month after a bad name day. Mae Dae. That's my name. That's what was printed on my name tag in bright blue letters that matched the visor. And so some customers, usually the young ones close to my age, would scream my name. "Mae Dae! Mae Dae! We're goin' down. Help us, Mae Dae!" And they'd fall all over the counter and cause ruckus and draw attention.

I was afraid they'd lose me my job. And I didn't understand none of it. Till I finally got the whole of the story out to Mrs. Price and she showed me some stuff on the internet about some May Day history and pilots and boat captains in trouble and poles with ribbons.

Now who would go and name their kid Mae when the last name would be Dae? My daddy couldn't help his last name. And I might have had a grandmother or aunt somewhere with the name of Mae, but my momma shoulda thought that one through.

If I ever have babies, I'll try out all their names first to be sure they don't have the same kind of mess I do.

Mr. Max wouldn't give me a new tag with just Mae on it, even though Mrs. Price came and asked. Something about City Burger policy. So the bullies kept on with their meanness. Mrs. Price told me a trick though. She said to play along and act like it was fun and they'd probably stop. I even came up with a line all by myself. The next time someone shouted "Mae Dae! Mae Dae! Help me," I'd said, "I'll help you get fries with that." And soon it died down.

But when Mr. Max got kicked out, Miss Manda heard a ruckus over it and she printed me up a new name tag that I pin to my shirt every shift. It just say MAE in all big blue letters and she even drew a butterfly by the M and a tulip by the E. And now no one ever comes into City Burger and screams "Mae Dae" at me. 'Cause they doesn't know my last name.

And cause Miss Manda care more about me than City Burger policy, she said.

I reach the back door of City Burger and go on into the office where I hang my bag in my cubby and take my MAE nametag out and pin it on my shirt. I'm grateful for my new nametag. I clock in with the cardboard slip that has Mae Dae on the top. I had lots of practice with this. I'm a little scared 'cause Miss Manda said they be gettin' a computer to clock in on soon. I'm not so good at the computers, but it hasn't happened yet, so I'm grateful.

I guess I'm just grateful all over today. For smooth hair and for a watch with lit-up numbers and for my job. Just a grateful kind of day. Grateful I didn't spot that green pickup, neither.

Eddie is out on the floor between the tables with his mop and bucket. I smile and duck my head so no one could catch me smilin'.

I go behind the bright blue counter and stand at my register. I trained and trained and trained. And I worked hard to learn it. I make mistakes sometimes, but I get it fixed right quick and don't get flustered as bad. Sometimes when I get flustered, I quick step away and do sodas. Fill one cup after another when we get busy. Or I go clean tables.

Cleanin' tables is my favorite cause it don't take no electronic smarts. Specially it's my favorite to clean tables if Eddie's cleanin' the floors at the same time.

And that day the green pickup came and that old man got out and came in and took what wasn't his, I was really grateful Eddie was there. I was gettin' that old man a refill and he used his wrinkled old hand and grabbed my behind. Right there in the restaurant in the open. Then he tried to take what wasn't his from my front side and Eddie came after him with the mop handle.

And that's how's come I got to meet a judge.

As another worker puts down the French fries and they sizzle and spit — I like that sound, the sizzle of the 'taters in the oil — the customers line up, so I have to concentrate as hard as I do on the bus. I take a few orders, and things go smooth like. I pay real close attention to their money, and I'm always glad when they just swipe their cards, then I don't gotta worry about giving out too many quarters or not enough dimes.

Things get busy all the sudden—always when City Burger gets busy, it happens all the sudden. Ain't no gradual about it.

So Miss Manda tells me go do sodas way before I have the chance to get flustered, then clean tables. Miss Manda good at tellin' those kinds of things. Mr. Max wasn't and he was a yeller.

I fine with this plan 'cause a minute ago some little child dropped strawberry milkshake all down under one table. Eddie'll have to clean it up once he's done emptyin' out the garbage bins.

And aside from bein' close to Eddie, cleanin' tables and deliverin' refills to the customers gives me the chance to scan the parking lot for that green truck. Chance to get away quick if I need to.

That day that nasty man did what he did, Eddie and I both got to meet the judge. City Burger sent some big smart lawyer to town to clean up the mess. 'Cause Eddie broke that man's wrist with the mop handle when he grabbed at me. And we could lose our jobs if that man won. Even though Eddie and me weren't the ones takin' things.

And I had to practice in a room with the lawyer. We pretended we was in a big fancy court, but it was just a room down at the Days Inn, and they had me put my gimp arm on top of the laywer's black briefcase. Said it was like the Bible. And I had to raise my right hand and repeat words like, "I, Mae Dae, promise to tell the truth." But those weren't exactly the words, 'cause the words were more big and smart. And then they shot questions at me until I got the answers just so.

I wipe the tabletop and seats off where that little child spilt his strawberry treat. It's so sticky, I have to go to the back and get a couple of fresh rags and refill the bleach cleaner. While I in the back, I straighten my visor again. Sometimes the sweat makes it ride down on my forehead.

When I get back to the table, there's Eddie, waitin' on me to finish so he can get under with the mop. He smiled big. My heart fills up, and I shy smile back to him, but hide under my visor some.

Only time I'd ever gone anywhere with Eddie was when that lawyer and his friends took us downtown to a real court to meet a real judge. I probably would've liked the ride in the backseat with Eddie, but the lawyer warned me the man from the green pickup would be waiting on us in the room. And that he'd probably be angry. So my knees bobbed up and down real fast on the way to the court. Eddie patted my hand and told me it was okay. That he had my back.

Eddie always is kind that way. And my knees settled down a little.

When we got in that room with the judge I'd been surprised she was a lady. I thought all judges were men. She was red-haired and freckled. I was so taken by her that I didn't pay much attention to the man from the green pickup. I did notice he had on a sling, though.

I wipe the table down with the fresh rag and wipe the seat off. A lady customer behind me pulls me away from Eddie and the messy table to get her a refill of Diet Pepsi. So I do that.

I fill the soda at the machine and think about that day in court as the soda hisses and hits the ice just so. That judge had a police officer bring a real Bible this time, and I let my gimp hand feel the leather of its cover. Then I remember gettin' scared, 'cause I know better than to tell any fibs while touchin' God's book. And I had to say again. "I, Mae Dae…" and more fancy words that just meant I was to tell the truth.

So help me God.

And I did. I told her what happened, and daggone it if I didn't start crying right there in the court. And she looked at me past her freckled nose and nodded and I think she believed me. And Eddie did so good and he swore to tell it like it was, too. And the lawyer said none of us or City Burger had to worry 'cause turns out the man in the green pickup was a pervert who'd grabbed a gob of other girl waitresses down at the diner and at the Quick-Stop.

So Eddie and me got to keep our jobs. And Miss Manda was glad City Burger didn't have to pay for that man's arm. 'Cause Eddie gave him what he deserved for trying to take what wasn't his to take.

After all that in court, on our way back to the lawyer's car, the judge saw us in the hallway. She'd taken off that heavy black gown and was in a pretty yellow dress with blue flowers. Didn't look like a judge at all, woman or not. She wanted to shake my hand. And then she put her arm around me and told me not to worry about that man no more. I listened to her words but I was more surprised at her pits. Guess it don't matter what color you are, Georgia heat ripens all pits the same.

As I bring that customer her Diet Pepsi, I scan the parking lot again. I freeze. My lip puckers. My knees go weak. 'Cause right there in the third parking space is a green pickup. I drop the soda all over the floor and stumble backward, right into Eddie. He looks at my face and looks out the window. And he stands there with me in the Pepsi mess, and I see the customer's big eyes, and then I watch out the window.

And Eddie watches with me with his mop handle standing tall. Until a mom and a couple of kids get outta that truck. I feel the breath go outta me and my insides unknot. Eddie wrings out the mop to get the mess before someone falls, and I pick up the cup, and promise the customer a brand new soda and a cookie for the trouble I caused.

When I turn to get the refill, Eddie whispers in my ear. "I got your back, Miss Mae Dae. I got your back." I smile and nod at him. A tear runs down my cheek and I quick brush it away on my shoulder.

Miss Manda must've seen what happened, 'cause after I get the cookie and soda to the customer, she wants to see me in the office.

"You okay, Mae?"

I nod.

"You sure?"

"I's just scared that man come back."

"He's in jail, Mae."

"I saw that green truck, Miss Manda. I thought he was back. Am I in trouble?"

"No. But please talk to me if you're scared or worried. I'll listen."

I nod again. "Can I go back to work, Miss Manda?"

"Why don't you go take a break? Out back. Get some fresh air for a few minutes, then start again."

I like that idea. I thank her and head out to the wooden picnic table behind the back door where the employees sit and smoke or sit and read while they take breaks. I don't usually come out here, 'cause I don't smoke and I don't care to read much, but Miss Manda's right. I need a moment.

And I's glad she had me come out 'cause I just saw Lacey Phillips pull into the parking lot in her shiny new red car her parents give her to go away to college in. Lacey got all As and a fancy scholarship to go learn to be whatever her smart brain could let her be. And she's a teaser, Lacey is. All smarts, but no heart, Mrs. Price said.

And I don't feel like no teasin' right now. She already know my last name, Lacey does.

I kick at a nasty cigarette butt with the toe of my tennis shoe. Eddie comes out to the dumpster and smiles at me. "You alright, Mae?"

"Yeah." I look away.

"After shift, you wanna get some yogurt before the Blue Line comes?"

Blue Line don't come until thirty minutes after my shift is over, so I got nothing better to do most nights than wait at a City Burger table. My heart thumps. It would be nice to wait at a Freezies' table across the street with Eddie. I nod my head.

"It's a date then." He grins big, and my heart goes from thumpin' to weak and my knees start to bob up and down.

I'd asked Mrs. Price long time ago if she thought I could ever have kids. 'Cause I'd like to try to be a momma someday. Not like my momma, but like Mrs. Price or Miss Manda kind of mommas. And I asked if those babies of mine would be like me. Not quite right. And I panicked a little when I asked her this, 'cause I didn't want to cause no babies no pain by makin' them like me.

She'd patted the couch next to her and put that big fat arm around me. And she told me to be patient and do some growin' up. And if I kept my nose clean and I chose a good strong husband who had straight-swimmin' sperm, there'd be nothin' to worry about.

And then she made me cry when she said what she said next. She told me that no babies on the planet would be as loved as the babies of Mae Dae. 'Cause I, Mae Dae, had the biggest heart of anyone she knew. And she cried with me and patted my hair and told me I was gonna do just fine with my big heart.

And that got me to dreamin' of a weddin' day. Me and some of the girls in the home would watch them reality shows of people gettin' married and gettin' fancy dresses. And mostly, out loud anyway, we'd poke fun and say how we'd *never* do any of that mess.

But in secret, after Mrs. Price told me what she told me, I dreamed.

I watch Eddie as he goes with empty trash bins back into City Burger. He smiles at me again before the door shuts behind him.

I close my eyes and let the Georgia sun warm my back. I rub down my left arm and feel the wavy and the weakness in the muscles. I straighten my visor again. And I dream of a weddin' day. A weddin' day when I'll say, "I, Mae Dae, take Eddie Morris to be my man."

'Cause Eddie Morris has my back. And he's never once tried to take what wasn't his to take.

And 'cause I do believe he a stand-up man with straight-swimmin' sperm.

The Sunrise Project

Thrust together on a school project, Drew and Sam have little in common—he the nerdy kid and she the rebel. And yet there is one bond that unites them, an unexpected kinship that grows in the light of dawn.

The assignment was simple enough. Mrs. Terrell wanted us to capture ten of the same "somethings" and document each one with a digital photograph complete with creative captioning. The class would assemble the collections into slide shows for two-thirds of our final grade. The project was due in two months. We could work in pairs or alone.

I planned to work alone.

"What will be your subject, Scott?" Mrs. Terrell walked between the rows of seats, jotting notes in her plan book.

"My dog?"

"Are you asking me or telling me?" Mrs. Terrell hated uncertainties.

"Telling you. I'll use my dog as my subject."

Mrs. Terrell eyed him and tapped her pen on the notebook. "There has to be a common theme through all the photos, Scott. I don't want ten random pics of your pooch." A couple of the girls snickered. Scott nodded and looked somewhat perturbed. Clearly, random pics was exactly what he'd had in mind.

She made her way up Scott's row. Some ideas were great, like the progression of a rose bud opening, a baby sibling's attempts at walking, the progression of a new addition on Mark Taylor's home. Others were bland, like Scott's dumb dog and MiKayla's hamster on its wheel.

"How about you, Mr. Adams?" She looked down at me over the top rim of her neon green readers.

This assignment was why I took this class. Since I was a freshman and saw the previous students' portfolios on the school's website, I'd known I would enroll in this class. I remembered hoping Mrs. Terrell didn't die before I had the chance to learn from her. She didn't die, and the only thing that changed was the amount of gray in her bun and the color of her readers.

"Sunrises from my backyard. I'll set up the tripod in the same location each morning, framed on one side by the branches of our neighbor's pine tree." I was sure she would be impressed because in three years I hadn't seen any portfolios of sunsets or sunrises.

The pen started tapping again and my heart sank a little. "Andrew Adams, you're going to get up before dawn each morning for ten days and photograph the sunrise?"

"It'll actually take longer than ten days. Some mornings there may not be clouds." *Oh, please don't shoot this down. Oh, please.*

"You're making this way too complicated, Andrew."

I have a knack for making things too complicated. I hesitated to answer.

"Your captions will be identical, will they not?"

"No sunrise is like any other. So the captions shouldn't be either." I hadn't thought as far as the captions. Now I was worried.

"I'll warn you now, there's a student each year who tries this and fails. They come to me a week later to change their topic."

Samantha Robbins piped up from one seat behind mine. "I can help him. I'm good at captions, and all of my subject matter ideas have been taken already."

I was taken completely off guard. I always worked alone. I spun around in my seat. She beamed. I did not.

She leaned half way across her desk, her wavy blonde hair scattered over her shoulders. "Anyway, it's *my* pine tree you're planning to use in each of your frames, isn't it?"

I turned back to Mrs. Terrell, ready to protest, but the old gal smiled. "That's a fabulous idea. I think, to keep the project on track, having a partner might be best."

A high-pitched "Sweet" came from behind me.

"Mr. Adams?" My teacher waited with her pen poised above her plan book.

I nodded in concession. "Wonderful."

Sam kicked the bottom of my seat. "See you bright and early, Drew."

THE NEXT MORNING, I slapped the alarm off my nightstand and swung my feet over the edge of the bed. I should have been excited.

Instead, I had to face Sam earlier than anyone should ever have to face Sam.

Overnight, my driving desire had changed from one of purely accomplishing the sunrise theme—and hopefully doing it well enough to submit it with a photojournalism scholarship application—to beating out every other student who quit on the theme in years past.

But now there was Sam.

I got good grades, and the teachers knew I did all my assignments. Occasionally, I'd get partnered with someone who didn't give a flip about anything and I ended up doing all the work anyway. Better than letting my grade suffer because the other half didn't turn their part in.

That's why I worked alone.

I grabbed my tripod and camera bag. I also tucked a notebook and a couple of pencils into my backpack so we could jot down ideas about captioning the shots as we waited for the clouds and sun angles to cooperate. I wanted to capture the sun at the same position every day and hope for a grand spray of clouds and light rays.

I wasn't sure what kind of grades Sam got overall, but she was unpredictable. Sometimes she'd go months without missing class. Sometimes she'd be gone three or four days out of the week for weeks in a row. It's been that way since fifth grade when her family moved into the house cattycorner from us. The edge of my backyard faced due east. Hers faced due south. A monster pine tree stood at the corner of her lot.

I grabbed a granola bar and a bottle of water and snuck out the back door so I wouldn't wake up Dad. Dew blanketed the grass, and it soaked my shoes through before I got to the edge of the yard. The first dim light of dawn broke beyond the pine. In the distance, a county road stretched east/west, and beyond the road farmland rolled as far as you could see. The farmers had worked the fields for the last two weeks, so I knew I wouldn't have to edit out tractors and combines.

I set my tripod up and lowered the legs so that the frame would show the pine and the farmland. The angle was such that the road couldn't be seen and no one would know unless a car happened to be passing.

Mom used to stand at our kitchen window as she readied our lunches before school. Sometimes during the year, she'd stare out the window and get lost in the view. "If I ever have to leave this place, I'll miss the sunrises the most."

I'd finally settled on the sunrise project last year when Mom left us because Dad couldn't keep his junk in his pants. We talk online, but she won't come home. Maybe for graduation, she said. I only stayed here to finish out my senior year. Maybe if she saw the project…

"Hey, dork!"

Sam came bounding from behind the tree, backpack swung over her shoulder. She carried a square of plywood under her arm. Her hair was done up in a bun and she wore baggy sweats and a t-shirt. I'd never seen her wear anything but nice clothes. She must've slept in that stuff.

I nodded to her and turned to the camera.

"I thought we could use the board to steady the tripod." She held it out for me.

"Thanks." I took the board and placed it under the tripod with instant success in stabilizing the three legs on the mole-infested yard. I swallowed my pride. "Good idea."

"You're welcome. So what's the plan?" She plopped down in the wet grass at my feet. The sky had lightened a bit, and I adjusted the exposure on the camera settings.

I explained to her my vision for the project, but hadn't thought of any captions yet.

"Well, that's nice." Her voice fell flat as she watched me tinker with the camera.

"Why, what?"

"Well, I was just thinking…"

My gratitude turned sour. "Thinking what? Mrs. Terrell pushed you into this with me to work on *my* idea."

"Jeez, it's my butt on the line, too. If this doesn't work out we'll both be scraping the bottom of the idea barrel for new topics."

"Okay, what is it?" I face her with hands on hips—like a sissy, now that I think about it.

"Well, if we captured the sun at its lowest today, then tomorrow we captured it a bit higher, and a bit higher the next day…" She stood up, framing the progression the sun would take as it rose higher in the sky with her arms extended, using her thumbs and forefingers as a guide. "You'd still capture ten sunrises, just a progression of sunrises. Much more interesting than showing the sun in a stationary position."

"That's gonna be really complicated."

But it was an excellent idea. My fears started to subside about the quality of work she'd put into the project. But when she spoke again, I got all flustered.

She grinned. "I hear you like to complicate things."

I shuffled my feet, kicking up dew drops onto the tops of my tennis shoes. "Well, at least we have that in common."

THE FIRST SEVEN mornings were successes. We got some great shots of the sun at the right progressions. Sam came up with some killer captions that captured the essence of the clouds and colors. Her captions gave our photos personality and were as good as the ones you see under photos displayed in an art gallery. I completed the edits on the "winning" shots from those days. I even sent a couple to Mom, but didn't hear anything back from her.

And not once had I woken up Dad.

We'd get the shots, retreat to our houses without saying much, and pass the day at school in silence. It was strictly a working relationship, which was the best thing to have if I couldn't work alone.

Then Sam didn't show up on the eighth morning.

I texted her several times, but there was no answer. The sun crept higher above the horizon, and it was almost time to start shooting. I was afraid to call because of her parents being asleep.

I did the best I could and packed up the gear. At least we'd decided to leave the board where it lay to make things easier.

At school, the seat behind me in photojournalism was empty. I texted her again from class, but got nothing.

Mrs. Terrell wanted updates. I told her everything was going fine. She looked over those green glasses at the seat behind me and I knew she doubted what I said.

"Do you need to change subject matter? It's not too late now, but it will be in a couple of days."

"No, not at all. We're all good." We'd worked so hard on this up until now and only had a couple of mornings left to go.

After school, I showed up on Samantha's front porch. After two rings of the doorbell and a knock, her mom answered the door. I barely recognized her.

The lady had been pretty, or at least I thought she had been. I didn't really see Sam's parents out in the neighborhood much. Then again, we also aren't exactly Mister Rogers' neighborhood either. Everyone pretty much always keeps to themselves.

"Mrs. Robbins, I'm sorry to bother you. Is Sam here? I missed her at school today." I was almost afraid to ask. She looked much thinner than I remembered. She had the same blonde hair and green eyes as Sam, but she was a mess, and she looked like she'd been crying.

"Sam!" Mrs. Robbins turned away from the door without a word to me, but she left it open. I didn't know whether to step in or to wait on the porch. So I waited on the porch. Cigarette smoke and something else I couldn't quite name wafted out of the open door. I waited as long for Sam to come to the door as I had for Mrs. Robbins.

Sam's appearance startled me more than her mother's did. She wore the same baggy clothes as she had that first morning in the back yard, but today she kept her arms crossed in front of her and her head down. Her hair hadn't been combed and she wouldn't look me in the eye.

"Hey, is everything okay? I tried to text you, but…"

"Yeah, I'm fine. I couldn't make it today. My mom needed me."

"Oh. I was just making sure…"

"I'll be there in the morning, okay? Sorry I missed today's shot."

"Yeah, that's okay. I got it done okay, but the angle may be a little off. We may want to try that one again." I glanced behind her to see her dad standing further in the living room, leaning against the wall with his arms crossed. "Get in here, Sam."

"Okay. In the morning. I promise." She backed away, head down, and slowly closed the door.

I stood there on the porch for a moment, trying to figure out what had happened. Maybe her mom was having a medical emergency. That would account for all the missed school in the past.

And then it hit me.

And I hoped I was wrong.

THE NEXT MORNING, I headed out a few minutes before dawn. Sam was already sitting next to the board in the grass. Her hair was pulled up in a bun and she had on different sweats and t-shirt.

"Hey." I started setting up the gear.

"Hey, Drew." She didn't look up. "I can help with this now, but I won't be at school today."

"Why not? Part of your grade depends on attendance."

"I know that. I just can't."

I took a couple of test shots and adjusted the settings. Sam stood and bumped me from behind the camera to frame in a few shots of her own.

I moved between her and the sunrise, which ticked her off enough that she finally looked up at me. Her left eye was a swirl of red and purple and a tiny cut split her eyebrow in the middle.

She realized I had seen her injury, even in the low light of the morning, and quickly ducked her head behind the camera again.

"Move, Drew. Or I'll send the whole school a picture of your crotch with pretty pink clouds all between your legs."

I moved to the side. She took a few more pictures, then retreated to her spot in the grass.

I had no idea what to say. My gut turned inside out and my hands started to sweat.

I should have worked alone.

And as soon as I thought that, I felt like a jerk.

"Are you okay?"

"Do I look okay?"

"Who did that to you?"

"Who do you think?"

"What can I do?" I stood there, knowing I was missing the perfect angle, but too afraid to care.

She pointed to the sky. "Just take the picture so I can go home."

I complied. I snapped off a few frames, and she stood to leave.

My feet moved my body in front of her without my head's permission. Then my mouth followed suit. "I don't think you should go home."

"Where do you think I should go?" Tears swelled, blurring the green in her eyes. "Back to your place? With your cheating dad?"

I took a step away from her. "You know about that?"

"Everyone knows about that, Drew. Email me the shot and I'll send you the caption."

I watched her stomp off until she disappeared through her back door.

I went home and threw up.

I UNDERSTOOD NOW why she missed so much. I tried talking to Dad before I left for school, but he didn't listen, his nose a few inches from his cell phone as always. I was ashamed of what he did to Mom, and even more so now that everyone knew. I guess everyone had probably known for a long time.

I thought about telling Mrs. Terrell, but I didn't want to be a snitch. I even came so close as to ask to see her after class, and then I had to make something up on the spot about the project that I already knew the answer to cover.

I really wished I'd worked alone. And I knew I was an insensitive freak.

I texted her again. She told me not to worry that she'd be there for the last photo in the morning.

But now I didn't care about the project nearly as much as I cared about what happened to Sam. And about how to stop it.

~

DAY TEN STARTED like most of the rest of them. Sam beat me again.

I set up the camera.

She took a few shots.

I corrected the settings.

She took a few more.

Her eye was a different swirl of colors, like the sunrises were different from minute to minute.

"I'm really sorry, Sam. I want to help. What can I do?"

"Nothing. There's nothing to do." She pointed to the sky. "It's time."

"I think we should call someone. Or talk to Mrs. Terrell."

She turned and shoved me from the camera and took the shot herself. When she finished, she faced me and said, "The last time someone called the police on my dad, I was put in foster care because my mom was a basket case. Please, Drew. Please don't do that."

I ran my hands through my hair and stifled a curse. I sat down in her spot in the grass. She sat next to me and put her hand on my knee.

"I'll be fine. I'll be eighteen soon. After graduation I'm moving away. I'll survive until then."

"I'm just so sorry. I feel so helpless."

She faced the wisps of purple and orange. In the growing light, her injury seemed to glow, and I tried not to stare. "The project's almost done. I'll get you the last caption this afternoon. But I won't be in class."

"They'll suspend you. Your grades won't count. You won't be able to graduate, and then…"

"I'll be fine, Drew."

And we finished watching the sunrise until the clouds burned off and time came for school.

~

SAM MADE good on her promise to finish the captions. When I got home the afternoon of the tenth day, a moving van pulled away from her drive, turned onto the county road we'd been so careful not to allow into the frame of our photos, and drove east. I never saw her again.

She didn't reply to my texts, and by the time graduation rolled around, the texts went undelivered.

Mom decided it was too painful to attend my graduation. I decided it was too painful to care whether she attended graduation. She had no comments, good or bad, about the photos Sam and I had worked so hard on. She must not have missed the view much; she certainly didn't miss me.

Dad came to the ceremony but was on his phone the entire time.

I kept Sam's secret. Maybe I shouldn't have. It kept me up at night and knotted my stomach inside out.

A week later, I received an email. In the subject line it read "Alternate captions."

Sam had attached a photo slide show, and I opened it. She'd chosen days one, nine and ten and reworked the captions.

Day One: The morning I may have found a friend.

Day Nine: The morning everything changed.

Day Ten: The morning I didn't say goodbye to my best friend.

I think about Sam a lot. I still take the camera out. The board is still in the grass. I take the shots and email them to her. Sometimes she sends back a caption.

Today, she sent a shot of a beach, the sun directly overhead, and a sign in the frame that read: Sand Dollar Beach, Big Sur.

I smile.

It's time for a sunset project.

Replacing Carrots

The passing of his wife leaves Matt the single daddy of two little girls. Little girls who, in addition to dealing with insufferable loss, are the target of their gossip-filled community. Can the weary father juggle it all in time to give his daughters one last Easter in the only home they've known before moving on?

att sat the dollar-store flashlight on the brown marble countertop and knelt on the tile floor in front of the bathroom cabinet. A black trash bag lay opened at his feet, a giant oval mouth waiting to swallow the last of Grace's unneeded items. He glanced over the toilet toward the small window. The bottom pane was covered with frosted Con-Tact paper to afford privacy and let in a bit of natural light. The top pane, its glass left bare, framed blue spring sky. A branch of one of the flowering crabapple trees he and Grace had planted in the landscaping of their brick ranch home ten years ago waved to him. Its dainty pink clusters were starting to give way to tender green leaves.

He'd avoided this task for some reason. This task in their master bathroom. The last of Grace's belongings not earmarked for Sophie or Sarah hid beneath the sink on her side of their double vanity. The black vanity cabinet she'd picked out during their pre-move-in remodel. The one she'd chosen while she and Matt had taken a break from planting all those flowering crabs.

Grace was still *everywhere*.

Her clothing, neatly folded in dresser drawers and hanging in pristine lines in the walk-in directly off the bathroom, had taken him weeks to face. Her floral-vanilla scent lingered on most of the pieces, and he didn't want to disturb that. The last lingering of her. But he'd found their five-year-old, Sophie, sitting on a pile of Grace's running shoes late one evening with her tiny face buried in Grace's favorite Northwestern U sweatshirt, and he'd had to start the process. Sarah, a couple years older, had clung to one of Grace's scarves, wrapping the purple polka dotted cloth around her neck and then smelling the edges of the silk. Cleaning the closet out had given them time to remember and grieve together, more so than the memorial service had.

It had also given the girls the safe space they needed—the three of them sheltered in the small walk-in, shoulder to shoulder to shoulder—to tell Matt of the hurtful words other kids in their classes at school whispered about their mother.

Things kids that age couldn't have come up with on their own.

Things kids that age would've overheard from careless carpool drivers or moms huddled in gossiping groups at a soccer practice.

It was all Matt could do after he got the girls to bed that night not to put his fist through the closet wall. And that was the night Matt decided they'd move. He'd let the girls finish the remainder of the school year and then be gone.

The next day, Matt had driven five counties over to donate the remainder of Grace's belongings. Five counties over where no one knew him and no one cared what had happened. Five counties over where the ladies in their small town didn't bother to shop. Where the chances of Matt seeing another woman walking around in his wife's clothes would be minimized.

And that next day he'd also visited the girls' school and demanded audience with their teachers. He'd explained what had been going on right under their noses and demanded something be done. The teachers placated him with "we'll keep an eye out" and "kids are cruel" and other such nonsense.

On his way back to the car, he'd spotted Meredith Baxter, a classroom aide, coming from the teachers' lounge. She floated between the classes, helping where needed, working a couple days at Elm Tree Elementary and the others down at Cora's Corner. She'd been in both his girls' rooms over the last couple of terms. Always kind. Always quiet. The girls seemed to like her and offered up comments like "Mrs. Baxter helped me with this," or "Mrs. Baxter said I did good today" several times a year.

Meredith had made eye contact with Matt, and her gaze darkened with a knowing. Of all the people in the county, Meredith would know why Matt was here today. Why he was so upset. She'd know because it was Grace's recent ordeal that had replaced Meredith's own gossip-worthy drama. When Grace had heard down at Cora's Corner that Meredith's husband had left her and their son for the prostitute he'd been seeing up in the city, Grace had been careful with her words. "A loss is a loss. None of our business how or why. That young mother deserves better treatment than that from the people in her life."

Matt and Meredith. Both victims of massive loss due to no fault of their own and the torrent of others' wicked words that followed.

He pressed down the rising anger and faced the cabinet to confront the last bit of his wife before he put the house on the market. Before he and their daughters would wave goodbye to the small brick ranch and crabapple trees and start a new life somewhere else.

He opened the wooden cabinet door and grimaced at the familiar squeak of the hinge. He'd promised her ages ago that he'd get out the WD-40 and take care of it. But things went downhill fast and the small annoyance was left to itself. He removed the first line of bottles. Shampoos, hairsprays and nearly empty nail polish remover. Those all went into the trash bag.

He reached back blindly, deeper into the cabinet behind the bottom bulge of the sink basin and pulled out another round of lotions—some of which he recognized as gifts he'd given her over the years—barely used or altogether unopened. He'd missed on those. The ones that didn't have quite the right scent. One of them had broken her out. He shook his head. She hadn't had the heart to throw them out. He tossed the lot of them into the trash.

He adjusted on the stool and felt further back into the dark, but his fingers didn't meet any other bottles or items. He aimed the flashlight's weak beam into the hollow to check the state of the cabinet and the underside of the sink. He didn't want to be surprised by a home inspection if something was amiss. Something that would cost a huge amount of money to fix or, more importantly, delay his exit from the tiny, gossip-filled burg.

The beam caught something at the back corner. Shiny. He hoped it wasn't a leak. He braced his shoulder against the edge of the cabinet frame and reached deep inside. His fingers met with plastic and he brought out a small bag of chocolates. Mostly gone, the bag had been folded around the remaining foil-covered pieces a couple of times.

He laughed and cried at the same time. Classic Grace. Hiding a stash in the bathroom. And hiding *herself* in the bathroom to escape the daily doldrums of motherhood—and likely Matt's mania over whatever new issue had crawled up his butt that day. He pictured her reaching into the cabinet, pulling out a few sweet pieces and sitting on the lid of the commode, savoring each bite as the house fell down around her. A moment to herself.

He unwound the bag and removed a square of chocolate. He peeled the foil and popped the morsel into his mouth. A little stale. No, a lot stale, but it seemed a fitting gesture to this last clean-out task. He looked down at the silver foil wrapper still in his hand. He turned it over and read "Savor New Beginnings" in flowy purple script.

He stared at the words and felt an anguish rise up to replace the dread he'd had at the beginning of this project. He wiped his mouth on the shoulder of his T-shirt and dropped the chocolates out one by one from their original package into the black trash bag.

It's incredibly difficult to savor new beginnings with stale chocolate.

~

THE BATHROOM CLEANOUT—THE chocolate, rather—had reminded Matt that the girls' Easter baskets weren't quite finished yet. He went to the attic access in the hallway and pulled on the rope to lower the rickety wooden steps.

When the girls were born, Grace's aunt had brought a giant wicker basket with a long, twisted handle filled with onesies, diapers and all things infant girl to the hospital. Sarah's had been purple, Sophie's pink. Grace, thrifty one she was, filled those baskets each year with Easter goodies. In between seasons, the baskets were wrapped carefully and placed in the attic.

Every spring season, after the Rabbit left town, Grace would buy certain items on clearance: plush bunnies or lambs, that plastic stringy grass that destroyed not one, but two vacuum cleaners, and sleeves of hollow plastic eggs to replace those broken or too-well-hidden. Grace's thriftiness had saved their small family a lot of money through the years, affording Matt the opportunity to continue his freelance editing business from home. The only thing they had to do when the next Bunny time came around was to buy fresh chocolates and the ever-famous hot pink marshmallow chicks.

He made his way to the far shelf where Grace kept the baskets and found them dutifully wrapped in opaque white plastic bags. He wrestled them down the steps and back to his bedroom where he could keep them from sneaky little girl eyes until Sunday came around. He unwound the twisty top ties and pulled the plastic from around the baskets, expecting to be greeted by stuffed animals or jump ropes or sidewalk chalk. Or something.

But they were empty. Save for a few strands of lime green grass, the purple and pink wickers were bare.

Then the timeline snapped into Matt's head. Grace had gotten sick, really sick, around the time the clearance sales would have been happening last spring. She never got the chance to get the girls' baskets prepped.

She'd been busy prepping for other things. Things like chemo treatments and goodbyes.

Matt turned and sat on the bed between the barren pink and purple baskets. Who knew the weight of Easter joys could be so heavy? With the realtor and inspectors coming later today and tomorrow, he'd have no time to make the trek to the city to shop in peace and get home before the girls' bus arrived. He'd have to face the all-too-familiar crowd at Cora's Corner and make do with whatever goodies they had in stock.

And what Cora's stocked was heavy in the gossip and light on the goodies.

CORA'S CORNER was just that. A tiny convenience mart situated on the corner of Main and 3rd Street and owned by Cora James, a now-elderly widow who refused to retire or sell the business she and her husband had built. The only source of essentials in Elm Tree, it served as a one-stop shop for milk, batteries, lottery tickets and all the verbal Elm Tree news one could ask for.

Matt pulled the minivan up to the curb in front of the store and took a deep breath. He'd been forced to park on the street because the back lot—all ten spaces of it—was filled with other minivans and SUVs belonging to mothers most likely tending to errands before school let out.

That's what Grace had done…

He entered the store, picked up a yellow plastic shopping basket and quickly scanned the place. Two semi-modern register counters guarded the front—one reserved only for Cora. The other for whomever she'd deemed worthy enough to help her man her mini-mart kingdom. Country music tumbled from gravelly speakers above. Seven or so aisles wide, three aisles deep. Usually the seasonal stuff was in the front, but this time Cora and Meredith had stocked the Easter bits in the middle. Probably wise. Make people walk past other shelves filled with made-in-China crap in hopes of padding the purchase.

On his way to the middle, his tennis shoe caught on an upturned floor tile. He remembered bringing the girls in here not long after Grace had passed, and Sophie had tripped on the uneven floor and toppled into a display of white powdered doughnuts. "Pick your feet up, little one," Cora had said as she handed both girls lollipops. "These floors are as old as I am." Cora had patted Matt on the shoulder and offered condolences and no judgment. She was about the only one in town that didn't have *that look*.

He made his way past two groups of yacking women, a couple of them seemed to recognize him. Whether paranoia or an accurate summation of their thought processes, Matt thought he recognized that look on several of their faces and hurried his step.

He found the endcap with the spring favors and tossed two bags of junky chocolates into his shopping basket. Those he would fill the plastic eggs with.

There was only one plush rabbit left, so he opted for two stuffed chicks to keep the fighting down. No hot pink marshmallow anythings, so he opted for yellow. He tossed in a couple malted chocolate eggs packed in milk cartons and egg-shaped bubble gum packaged in mini egg cartons. Last year, the girls had played with the packaging more than they had enjoyed the contents.

One shelf held the better chocolates…Truffles and caramel-filled joys that Grace loved but the girls hadn't developed a taste for yet.

But the carrots caught his eye. Fancy cone-shaped chocolates wrapped in orange foil from their tips to the tops where green foil served as carrot tops. Four to a package and several packages left, likely because they were more expensive than the kid-friendly junk. He didn't care, though. This was to be their last Easter in that home, and a little splurging was okay. And shopping here saved him gas money and time versus driving to another town to find this exact stuff.

He wanted to linger through the endcaps and think the basket fillers through a little more, but he could sense the other shoppers' presence and glares pressing in on him.

He tossed two packs of carrots into the basket and headed for Cora's checkout.

Hold it together, Matt. Just get it done and get home.

As she rang up his items, he noticed the bulging of arthritis around her knuckles and wondered how much longer the old gal could hold out. She smiled sweetly at him as she rang up the last fuzzy chick. She winked and tossed in two lollipops, free of charge. "Tell the girls I said hello."

He tried to smile back. "Will do and thank you." Matt shuffled and looked over his shoulder. Several women had lined up behind him, all taking peeking turns around each others' shoulders to get a good look at the pathetic widower buying Easter at Cora's Corner. He gathered the plastic bags and, remembering to pick up his feet, hustled to his van, nearly knocking Meredith Baxter into the entrance door in the process.

MATT WATCHED from the spare bedroom window—his office window—as the realtor made a phone call in the driveway before pulling away. He hoped the call was to a prospective buyer and not to the gossip brigade. He prayed that the house wouldn't sit on the market for ages. Who in their right mind would want to move to Elm Tree?

He looked down at the paperwork still in his hand. The pen had weighed a hundred pounds as he drug the nib across the signature line of the listing agreement. Agreeing to abandon the home he and Grace had started their family in.

Shake it off Matt. The girls will be home soon.

He shoved the documents into the desk drawer and went to his bedroom.

Matt filled the leftover plastic eggs with random chocolates and, for good measure, added quarters and dimes into some of the eggs. He unwrapped a blue foil-covered treat and popped it in his mouth as a reward for finishing the eggs. He winced. Grace's stale chocolate was better than this stuff. He guessed it was more the novelty of it than the culinary experience.

He started unpacking and untagging the basket goodies, dividing up the chicks and marshmallows and bubble gums. He tucked one box of fancy carrots in front of each chick in each basket and stood back to assess his efforts.

Something wasn't right. The baskets seemed shallow, like the chicks were struggling to see over the wicker rims.

He arranged a few plastic eggs around the chicks and carrots. That didn't work either.

Grace was so good at this kind of stuff. Why did his—

Plastic grass, stupid.

He cursed under his breath. This would mean another trip to Cora's tomorrow. He remembered seeing the grass. Right there on the endcap. But he was too busy worrying about the stares from the ladies in the store to process the plastic grass shreds staring up at him from the shelf.

The squeal of the bus brakes startled him. He scooped the filled plastic eggs into the wicker baskets and hid them under a quilt on the floor of the walk-in closet. He made his way to the front door to greet his daughters, but Sophie wouldn't come in. Sarah dropped her backpack in the grass and stood with her arms wrapped around her little sister and looked at the house toward Matt.

He met the girls in the yard. Sophie looked up at him, tears streaming down her freckled face. He brushed her brunette hair away from her wet cheeks. He kissed Sarah on the top of her head. He didn't have to ask what had happened. He knelt and put his arms around both of his children and held them.

His little girl had held it together long enough to get home. Until she couldn't hold it together any longer.

AFTER A FROZEN PIZZA DINNER, Matt gave the girls the lollipops from Cora. The tears had dried, but the stories that had toppled out over the pepperoni slices broke his heart. He'd had no appetite to join them for dinner, so he listened and tried to comfort.

Homework, baths, pajamas, and bedtime stories dotted the rest of the evening. When he shut the girls' bedroom door, he went to his office to try to work, but the brain cells wouldn't fire. He'd taken on fewer and fewer jobs per month since Grace's death. He had to find a new normal. A new rhythm. And soon.

Or Easter baskets would be the least of his worries.

He shut the laptop, went to his bathroom, and closed the door. He stared at himself in the oval mirror above his vanity. He never looked at himself in Grace's mirror. Not after all these months—and likely not before. They each had their sides of the sink. He looked old. Older than he'd looked even last week. He didn't want his girls to see him like this. He had to pull it together.

Grace hadn't wanted the girls to watch her downward spiral, either. She'd experienced that as a ten-year-old when her mother, though her diagnosis slightly different, had wasted away week by week, month by month until she wasn't Grace's mother anymore. Her mother had become something else. Grace had pulled it together, or so Matt thought. He'd seen her rally and thought she was in the fight to the end—or maybe all the way to remission. He'd let hope sneak in. That was a dangerous thing to do.

But Grace really hadn't pulled it together. She had pulled together an exit plan. One that she was at peace with, but he didn't approve of. And somehow, the entirety of Elm Tree sensed Grace had ended her own suffering before the cancer could.

And his little girls, though spared the visuals of a deteriorating mother, were handed instead the doubts and ridicule of an entire community.

You should've seen this one coming.

He splashed water on his face and patted dry with a hand towel. His stomach growled from grief and the lack of dinner finally catching up with him. Real food didn't sound good, nor did he have the energy to cook.

He took a few steps into the walk-in and peeked under the quilt. He couldn't stomach any more of the generic egg-filler. He brushed the plastic eggs aside. The brightly colored orange carrots greeted him, and he picked up a box. All four carrots neatly displayed against a cardboard garden background.

He walked six steps to the toilet, closed the lid, and sat down. He rationalized that he'd have to rework the baskets anyway, so he'd open the remaining box of carrots and split them evenly between the girls. He'd try out this one tonight. See if the fuss is worth the extra cost.

He opened the box and carefully unwrapped the first carrot-shaped goody, no more than three inches long, and popped the whole thing in his mouth. Brand-name chocolate. Not stale. Smooth and sweet, it glided down the back of his throat like a soothing medication.

Matt took time to smell the second one before he unwrapped it. He ran the carrot under his nose like a fine cigar. This was no ordinary chocolate. This was heaven. He allowed it to melt in his mouth. Slowing down his urge to devour. Trying to enjoy.

As it turned to liquid in his mouth, he thought of Grace doing the same thing with the chocolates under the sink. And he understood. He wept in between swallows as he finished off the other two carrots.

He stood, feeling a bit better but not quite at peace and decided that, since another trip to Cora's was imminent for the fake grass anyway, he'd replace *both* boxes of chocolate carrots tomorrow.

He retrieved the second box from the purple wicker basket and returned to his throne.

To savor and sob as the crabapple branch brushed against the window pane.

~

AFTER PLACING two reluctant little girls on the school bus, Matt rushed down to Cora's Corner. Maybe this early in the morning the busybodies were still in their housecoats, sipping steaming coffee and scrolling Facebook and not on their way to the convenience store. He'd beat the busiest time and have plenty of time to tidy up before the home inspection this afternoon.

He parked the van in the front again, closer to the checkouts, and behind a beat-up blue Intrepid. The minimart had been open only fifteen minutes. Surely this would go smoothly.

Cora greeted him warmly. He thanked her on behalf of the girls for the lollies. Meredith was counting the cash in her register till and nodded at him quickly, then looked away.

He grabbed a yellow shopping basket and went to the endcap housing the Easter supplies. Much to his dismay, the back aisles were already bustling with women; some the mothers of other kids in his girls' classes, and a couple of older women he recognized from around town.

Matt didn't realize at first, but his feet had frozen in place and he was blocking the path of a couple of ladies. What could they all possibly need all the time from this hole-in-the-wall store? None of them had shopping baskets. Only a couple of them held any needed item in their hands. They were just…there.

"Excuse me." One of the ladies touched his elbow and nudged her way past Matt. He shuffled his feet toward what remained of the Easter goodies. She reached for that last plush rabbit, sized him up and said, "I guess this all falls on you now, huh? A shame what Grace did." She walked toward two other women and whispered something to the small group.

Matt squared up to the endcap, his ears burning and face

flushed. He tried to focus on the task in front of him. Two simple things. Then go home.

Don't forget the basket grass.

Replace the carrots.

He put two packs of lime green grass into his shopping basket. He glanced around. A second group of ladies had gathered to watch and whisper. Or maybe they were waiting on him to move.

He turned back to the shelves. The cardboard display that held the boxes of chocolate carrots was empty. As were several other cardboard displays. The Easter loot had been looted in one short day. He moved bags of crappy chocolates around and dug behind picked-over Peeps.

No carrots.

Panic seized him. He'd already pictured his girls' faces and their giggles over the novelty chocolate. He'd planned to tell them that their mother preferred this kind over the egg filler kind. He'd planned a whole momentous memory over those carrots for Sunday morning after the Bunny came.

A few hollow chocolate rabbits stared at him with their sideways sugar eyes. He didn't want to give the girls hollow rabbits. But they would have to do.

He tossed two bunnies into the basket and headed for the checkout. The woman who'd made the rude comment followed with the stuffed plush. The other women nonchalantly followed suit until they were all lined up, peeking around shoulders as they had the day before. Matt placed the basket on Cora's counter. She was much slower today, and her fingers could barely grab the items from the basket. Between the first two register beeps, he could hear whispers.

He turned to the ladies behind him, and the first two women startled a bit and shifted their gazes, one to the floor, one to the ceiling. Cora rang up the last two items. Four beeps total.

"Is there something I can help you ladies with? Something you can't reach on some top shelf somewhere? Something you'd like to *know?*" Matt heard his voice before his brain processed what he was doing. He wanted to stop, but blinding anger overcame him.

One lady went pale. One lady, an older one, muttered, "Well, I never."

"I never either," Matt yelled. The loss of control went from his vocal cords to his feet. He turned to the counter, Cora's pale blue eyes wide behind her glasses, and he jumped on top of the checkout to get a better view. He stood up straight, towering over the gathering at the front of the store.

"I never had to care for two kids on my own. Girls, even. I know nothing about raising girls. I never lost a spouse before. I never cooked this much in all my life." Matt looked down at Cora, who'd nudged his leg. She was smiling. Nodding.

And holding up the corded intercom system's mouthpiece. "Just press in on that button right there."

Matt took the device, pushed the button on the side and heard a gravelly spark through the speakers in the ceiling. "I never—" His voice was so loud and filled Cora's Corner from front to back, it startled him and the line growing at the checkouts. He looked around. Meredith nodded. Cora nodded. The other ladies gaped in disbelief.

"I never ever thought a small community like Elm Tree could house such wicked people. Grace sure didn't. She loved this place. How dare you all huddle and whisper. Your kids hear you, you know. They repeat the awful things you say about my Grace. Their mom. Your kids are listening to your rumors and theories." He paused, took his finger off the button for a moment before continuing.

"You've no idea what it's like. You've never lost someone like I did. Like my girls did. All I want to do is have a peaceful Easter. Make this one special for Sophie and Sarah. And I forgot the grass. And I ate all the fancy carrots last night after my girls went to bed weeping. And all I wanted was to replace the stupid carrots. And you all… You all will never know what it's like."

He shuffled his feet on the counter before jumping down. He handed Cora the mouthpiece. Tears wet her cheeks and the kind old woman threw two handfuls of lollipops into his bag with the Easter grass and cheap rabbits. Meredith had left her register with its line of ladies and went out the front door.

He heard sniffles in the line behind him. He picked up the bag and looked back again. The lady from the aisle clutched the tiny rabbit to her chest. "Cry. Laugh. Post it on Facebook. But remember my daughters, please. Because you have no idea."

Meredith met him at the driver's side of his van. She'd been crying. "I'm sorry for your loss." She held out a plastic sack. He opened his door and placed his sack from Cora's inside and took the bag from her.

He looked in it. Two boxes of orange foil-covered chocolate carrots. "For your girls. Take them, please."

"I can't. These are for your son's Easter." Now Matt's face was wet.

She brushed the dampness from her cheeks and gave a little laugh. "Are you kidding me? I drove five counties over to Target to buy those for my middle-of-the-night meltdown stash." She returned to her car and pulled out another sack. She handed him a third box of carrots.

"Sounds like you need to replace *your* carrots too."

Matt wiped his face on his sleeve and took Meredith's gift. "I guess so. And thank you."

"No problem." Meredith returned to her register and the line of onlookers.

Matt sat behind the wheel and calmed himself before taking off. He opened one carrot box and removed just one chocolate, unwrapped it. Smelled it. Then popped the whole thing in his mouth. He debated whether the two kind souls in Elm Tree were worth sticking around for.

With time—and chocolate—he may be able to figure it out.

The Gatherer

In Cantleberry Cemetery, the shade falls heavily on forgotten headstones. For Aimee, this place is sacred—a place of quiet kinship. The kind of closeness she never had growing up.

*A*imee sat in the dew-soaked grass next to Mr. Carter. She loved the ancient twisted oak tree and the rolling view of the headstones into the distance. From her vantage point, she could see the grave markers progress from simple to ornate to shiny marble, as each decade the dead required more land.

And for as long as Aimee had been visiting the graveyard, Mr. Carter and his family never had any visitors. No flowers or Memorial Day wreaths had ever been placed for them, nor for the plots surrounding, as these folks passed so long ago that their children were probably buried on down the hill.

But she'd taken over the job of visiting the Carters as if she knew them.

She imagined Mr. Carter, Clarence Carter, a kind old farmer, loving husband—just like the headstone read—and devoted father. She imagined his wife, Mrs. Elaine Carter, to be a doting mother who would do anything for her children.

The breeze rustled through the oak, and the hefty branches creaked like an old door in need of oil. Aimee traced the names on the concrete stone with her fingertips and imagined herself as their dutiful daughter, tending to their final resting place.

Aimee never knew her parents. The Carters were the fourth couple in the graveyard whose family she imagined being a part of.

Foster placements carried no fond memories for Aimee, but Mr. Gaines, the flower shop owner, had given her a chance, and she'd found her peace in Ruby's nursery with the flowers and in Cantleberry Cemetery among the rows of long-forgotten souls.

From the edge of the property a lawnmower started, and Aimee knew she'd be in the way. And it was time for her shift. She stood and brushed some of the damp off and gave the Carters' headstone a loving pat. "I'll be by tomorrow morning. And I'll have a surprise for you both."

～

AIMEE STRAIGHTENED the tools and swept the floor, careful to pick up the discarded scraps of ribbon that were long enough to suit her needs. She twisted the open sign to closed and locked the door to Ruby's Roses. Ruby's had lived in the brick building on the corner of Main Street for three of Aimee's lifetimes. The family-run flower shop was the only one in Cantleberry. That was good news for the owners, but quite overwhelming when several area residents passed away in a short time.

In the last few days, two elderly ones had passed away, and a couple had died in a car accident. At least they didn't have any little kids depending on them. Their son was grown, from what Mr. Gaines had told her.

Aimee much preferred tending the greenhouses on the edge of town over the shop, but busy times called for all hands on deck to assemble the sprays and wait on the customers ordering afghans, windchimes and garden benches.

Since leaving the graveyard early that morning, she'd arranged casket sprays and planters. She'd also delivered a van full of arrangements to the funeral homes, returned to the store and reloaded it with another batch. One family had requested the flower shop deliver the freshly cut flowers to the gravesite for an evening service, and then she would be free to go home. At twenty-three, Aimee was the most trusted employee Mr. Gaines currently had on staff. For six years now, she showed up, did her job and didn't cause him any trouble.

Aimee sped out to the newer part of the cemetery where maintenance had already mowed and trimmed, and the gravediggers had already set up for the funeral service. A green tarp covered the mound of dirt next to the rectangular pit. The crew placed the finishing touches on the site and left. She didn't know the cemetery staff's names, even with as much time as she spent walking the grounds. She tried to avoid the living.

She drove up to the site on the gravel lane. She had to hurry before the family and friends of the deceased arrived. Folding chairs covered in navy fabric lined the perimeter of the site under a white canopy. She unloaded the fresh-cut flower arrangements one by one.

She left the casket spray of red and white carnations with a blue ribbon at the base of the podium, as the hearse had not arrived with the casket yet.

A group of uniformed men gathered with rifles a few rows away. One man had a bugle.

Aimee finished unloading the van and stepped back to make sure the site looked as nice as possible. She thought about going home, but drove the gravel lane back to watch the procession with the Carters.

She leaned against the oak and watched men in suits and women with hankies fill the folding chairs. With the distance from the older section of the cemetery to where the military burial was taking place, the people, props and vehicles looked just the right size for a dollhouse.

She couldn't hear the minister, and she could barely make out a quartet of men singing a cappella. *Amazing Grace*, maybe. A few minutes more and two military men folded the flag from the casket and handed it to a lady in the front row. Then the guns.

Aimee covered her ears and ducked. The noise startled her to the core, even though she'd known the shots were coming. She wasn't prepared for her own reaction, though, as tears flowed down her cheeks and her stomach quivered.

She put a hand over her mouth to stifle a sob, but knew that the attendees couldn't hear her. They probably hadn't even seen that she was standing up the hill.

That is, they didn't hear her until a hand reached out for her shoulder and made her squeal. Heads turned from across the cemetery, and Amy scampered behind the tree.

A young guy stood behind the tree holding a weed-whacker in one hand, his other hand over his mouth to stifle whatever sound he was about to make.

"What are you doing here?" she whispered.

"I could ask you the same thing. I'm doing my job." He held up the trimmer. "I thought it rude to run the thing during the ceremony, so I was just watching."

She roughly wiped the tears from her face, leaving her cheeks burning. "Well, you should be able to get back to it soon." She crossed her arms around her and peeked around the tree. Everyone had gone about the business of grief and she was glad her commotion hadn't disrupted things too badly. The grieving family threw flowers from the arrangement onto the casket as it was lowered.

"I'm sorry I startled you. You okay?"

She nodded.

"You sure? Did you know him?"

Lawn Guy stared down the hill as the hearse pulled away, followed in spurts by other vehicles.

"No. I didn't know him." Aimee wished he'd leave already, but a quick glance around showed he still had several rows of trimming left to do.

"I'm Blake, by the way." He reached out his hand. "I just started here today."

"Aimee." She didn't offer her hand, and would forget his name soon enough. She leaned against the tree hoping he'd get the hint.

"Well, see ya round. Maybe."

She turned and watched him walk three rows back and down. He looked down the hill and when the last people entered their cars, he started the trimmer.

AT DAWN, Aimee was back at the cemetery. She drove by the gravesite from last night's ceremony and got out of the car. The green tarp and folding chairs were gone. The canopy tent broke the horizon a dozen rows to the south for the next burial.

She glanced around and when she was satisfied no one was watching, she knelt by the fresh mound of dirt and started gathering.

After every burial, the leftover flower arrangements that weren't claimed by someone were dumped onto the dirt mounds—a ritual Aimee never quite understood.

In the nursery, Aimee grew those very same flowers from seedlings. She watered them, pruned them and clipped them. She delivered them to Ruby's Roses where they were tweaked and tucked into arrangements of all sorts

Most of them ended up in the cemetery as throwaways.

Just like her.

For years, Aimee had come to the cemetery early after a burial and gathered the castaway flowers, but she never took them *all* away, though. Many of the stems she arranged neatly, tied them with a single scrap of the leftover ribbon bits from the store, and tenderly laid them back on the mound. For some reason, she didn't like the haphazard sight of strewn flowers. Sometimes, even the containers were thrown onto the grave. Aimee always picked those up and discarded them on her way to work.

But *some* throwaways she did take. Tiger lilies were her favorite, followed by simple white carnations. Most of the time, the roses were thrown into the ground and lowered away with the casket or taken home by someone. But, occasionally, she'd find one or two. Like today.

When she had an armful of various sizes and colors, she put them on the floorboard of the van and drove up the hill to the oak tree.

"I told you I'd have a surprise for you today." She spoke softly as she patted the Carters' headstone. She leaned a white rose against Clarence's name and a red rose against Elaine's. "And since you guys got treated to roses today, how about we share the rest with the neighbors?"

One by one, Aimee placed flowers along the row of weathered headstones until she ran out. She made note of whose turn it was next, and tomorrow, after today's burial, she'd start where she'd left off.

She walked back two rows and took in the sight and smiled. The discarded blooms got a second chance to brighten an otherwise bleak existence on the hill under the old oak tree.

Behind her she heard the familiar buzz of the weed-whacker. She turned to see Lawn Guy working the rows.

He'd been watching her.

SEVERAL WEEKS PASSED, and Aimee continued to visit the graveyard, gather when she could and keep her shifts for Ruby's. Then she broke her left ankle—a freak accident involving an unsupervised child at the flower shop who'd left his toy tractor in the middle of the floor. Aimee came out with an armful of greenery and wiped out.

A cast and crutches were not conducive to nursery work, nor to graveyard visits, though she tried. She could drive, but gathering the flowers was nearly impossible.

She visited the Carters two days after.

"I'm sorry I'm late." Aimee sat on the ground, knowing good and well it would take her quite an effort to get up from that position. She spilled out the story and frustration to her ever-patient friends. She glanced down the hill and noticed three more fresh graves in the newer section. All covered with colorful castaways. She put her head on her knees and sobbed.

"Do you know these people?"

For the second time that month, in nearly the same spot, her sob turned into a frightful squeal. She looked up to see Lawn Guy standing over her.

"Blake, remember?"

She nodded. She remembered, even though she'd tried not to.

"I only ask because you seem to be here quite a bit. I mean, I've even given you privacy a few times and done the graves further down or over there so I wouldn't disturb you, but you always seem to be here." He dropped the trimmer in the grass and sat facing her.

Aimee wanted to run away and hide. Or fight.

Or both.

"I don't know them." She gritted her teeth.

"Why do you come?"

She shrugged. "Why not?" She made eye contact with him for a split second, then looked away again.

"Why are you crying? Does it hurt?"

"No. My ankle doesn't hurt."

"Then why cry?"

"Why not?" This was getting old and she tried to wriggle the crutches around to stand. Blake jumped up, steadied the crutches and helped her to her feet, which started a fresh wave of tears as it reminded her that she was nearly helpless in this state.

"You bring them flowers."

"Yeah, but I won't be able to for a while." She waved one of the crutches in the air.

"And you don't know them? The Carters?"

"No. I'm not from around here. Not even a distant relative. I don't know any of these people." She tapped the trimmer with the end of the crutch. "Don't you have work to do? Like down in the newer section?"

Blake picked up the trimmer. "Probably. But I prefer the view from up here, so I ask for this section whenever I can." He smiled warmly at her and she felt that blasted quiver in her stomach, but this time it wasn't from gunfire.

~

DESPITE THE PAIN in her ankle, which she'd lied to Blake about on the hill the day before, she drove to the gravesite at dawn.

All his questions irked her. Why this and why that. She didn't really know why. She felt a closeness up on the hill with the Carters. But she didn't know *why*.

She pulled the van to the side of the gravel lane and decided not to sit down in the grass this time. She hobbled on crutches to the front of the stones; the pain in her armpits hurt nearly as bad as the pain in her ankle.

When she faced the front of the headstones, she nearly fell over and dropped one of the crutches.

The Carters had a bouquet of tiger lilies between their names. And all down the row in both directions as far as Aimee could see, each headstone had a single white daisy tied with a tiny blue ribbon.

She looked over the rolling hill, shading her eyes from the rising sun and noticed that the three fresh graves from yesterday had been cleaned of their discarded flowers. She spotted two more graves, side by side, in the newer section, and someone kneeling between the mounds, gathering the flowers and straightening the chaos.

Then that someone, arms full of long stems and colorful blossoms turned toward her and walked up the hill.

It was Blake.

Along the way, he would lay a flower or two on a grave that had none. By the time he reached her he had three roses left. She hopped backward out of his way and watched in silence as he placed a white rose for Clarence and a red rose for Elaine.

He handed her a pink one, which she instinctively put up to her nose to inhale the sweet aroma.

"Why are you doing this?" Every time she saw Blake, she was crying. Every single time.

"Those two down the hill. There together?" He pointed to the side-by-side mounds. "Those were my parents. They died a few days ago in that car crash out on Route 58." He shifted his feet. "I took this job to be close to them in some weird way, I guess."

Aimee couldn't speak. She didn't bother wiping away the tears. They stood in silence for a few minutes. Blake knelt in front of the headstone.

"And these two here. These two that you've been keeping company all this time? These are my great-grandparents."

Aimee's head spun. She looked Blake in the eyes—the kindest eyes she'd seen in quite some time. She started to apologize, but he stopped her.

"Let's try this again." He stood and held out his hand in greeting. "I'm Blake. Blake Carter. And it's so very nice to meet you."

All the Knitted Unicorns

The employees of Save-N-Shop never dance with glee when they see old Mrs. Halston pulling in with her list of demands regarding her forever unsold handmade toys. But young Kerry learns a valuable lesson—and maybe spots a new direction for her life—when those toys bridge the gap of loneliness.

slammed my rusted blue Bug into park in the third spot in Save-N-Shop's employee lot. The lot has six spaces and occupies the far corner of the main lot, which holds about forty cars if the asphalt held up through the Indiana winter, and twenty if it didn't. But we only ever need ten spots to be functional for parking. Since things calmed down a year ago, we're never that busy.

The employee spots are for the manager, two clerks—I'm the second clerk, thus the third spot—Deli Guy Greg, and two stock folks. A couple of oak trees, aggravated at the intrusion of their solitude in the corner of the lonely lot, drop limbs on our cars in the winter, toss twigs in the spring, spit their acorns in the late summer, and poop leaves in the fall. They want us gone. After my shift, I'll have acorns to deal with. Bright blue sky and crisp breeze, though, so I'll likely take my lunch break at the battered picnic table under the oaks. I promised them I wouldn't talk much, though. They could go about their tree-ness.

I don't usually talk to trees. But I think after the last couple of years, lots of people do lots of things they normally wouldn't. Like talking to plants.

I'm on time today, but barely, so Steve won't be on my case too much. I told him as much as I do around here, I should get the first clerk spot, since Savannah is always late—later than me—and I'm his go-to acting assistant manager. Putting out fires, triaging whining customers, and unsticking registers and payment machines while he spends most of his day like a king in a high tower behind his only slightly elevated glassed-in overlook in the front corner of the store. From there, he's got a good view of the entire establishment, and watches us and the customers wander like avatars in a slow-moving video game. He may answer the phone in between his bites of pizza rolls or egg salad or whatever Deli Guy Greg put out fresh that morning.

I shuddered a bit. We knew what Steve ate by the color of the stains on his blue necktie and the bits that escaped that track and gobbed up around the buttons in his white oxford.

I grab my smock from the backseat and slip the apron top

around my neck and over my t-shirt and jeans. I pull my straight brown ponytail out from captivity and check myself in the mirror. Which is new for me. Our clientele doesn't care what they look like, let alone what I look like, as long as our hands are clean.

But as of about last week when that guy started coming in every couple of days, I found myself making sure things were a little more on point. Light blush. Light eyeliner. That's about it. I'm pretty simple. But still.

That evaluator fellow would fill one of our lime green shopping baskets with only healthy-ish stuff. He was polite and soft spoken. Jet black hair and blue eyes. And about five years my senior. As I checked him out, both his groceries and his muscled physique, he'd sometimes ask where a certain business was or the hours of our local post office.

His job was to check up on the counties. Rural ones like ours got to go last. But we'd been fairly self-sufficient to begin with, so the government put us at the bottom of their to-do list. And for a government employee, he wasn't stuffy. He dressed in jeans and a simple collared shirt. No stains down the front like most of the men I see all day. And when he left my register, the faint hint of his cologne would linger and make me near drunk.

The only two non-post-pandemic business questions he'd asked me ran through my head over and over again. "Where's the St. Venue Children's Hospital from here?"

First, that's not even in our county and second, he had a GPS. And Google. So I got my hopes up that he enjoyed chatting with a lowly grocery store clerk and I answered him.

The second one: "What's up with all those unicorns?" And the crooked little smile he had on his face and the sparkle in those ocean eyes. Wow. I'd stammered and stuttered as I answered him, but wow.

And he bought one. Our first knitted unicorn sale came from the money stuffed deep in the right front jeans pocket of the most handsome guy this side of the Mississippi.

So today, if he were to restock his salad and bagels, I'd decided to muster the courage to ask him his name and how far he'd traveled to give our good old Covort County the once-over.

I straightened the front of my smock and my nametag. Last year Steve finally realized I'd likely stick around for a bit and swapped out my hand-Sharpied "Kerry" sticky note with an engraved one with pin-back closure and the mom-and-pop's emblem—a brown paper grocery bag with green dollar bills spilling from it. Most of the temp help he'd hired during the panic buying frenzy of Covort County went on with their college plans or back to being stay-at-home parents. The Save-N-Shop employment got them through until things settled. But I stayed.

Don't know sometimes if that was the right decision. According to the parental figures in my life, I'm now wasting my life because some bug got me off track of my high-end nursing field dreams.

I came to Save-N-Shop when college stopped and was still able to do good without the stress. I saw what those 24-hour shifts did to Sue and Amara, the gals that graduated just three years before I would have. Just not cool. Not cool.

So I stayed. I walked across the rubber-coated pressure-plate that swung open the glass entry door nearly every day since Steve and Gary begged us all on social media to help them stock shelves and take care of our ever-growing old folks' shopping needs. Well, sometimes, when I was the one that opened the store, I had to jump up and down on the mat. Gary has some mad mechanical skills, and Steve decided to save money and not upgrade to one of those cool high-tech door sensors. "'Cause, Kerry, once you get her movin', she swings the doors open just fine."

"Yeah," I'd argued. "Until old Mrs. Struthard can't get out the door and she breaks a hip jumping up and down in front of it." The old guys shrugged and went about their business. But really. It was fun for the kids to jump on the plate to open the doors. Not so much for the elderly.

"Hey, Freckle-Kinned Kerry. Good morning my dear." Gary, in his white deli apron—must be a new one because there are no hints of stains on the front—greets me this way each day. Every day. I do have freckles, but I have no idea what a Freckle-Kin is. But Gary's old. Like a Dad-almost-granddad type, so I allowed him the nickname.

If Steve tried such a thing, we'd have a sternly worded conversation. I've been a faithful Save-N-Shop employee long enough to be allowed one sternly worded conversation with Steve a month. Aside from being on the cheap side and a slob, I've come to think of him as family-once-removed. Gary, too.

Even Savannah. Even though she's just a bit too needy. Like now. She'd walked in and started up her register and immediately asked if I'd deal with the first customer of the day. I turned back toward the parking lot.

A dark green Buick Lesabre was pulling into the handicapped spot. Right on time. It was Tuesday, after all.

"Savannah, what if I'm not here some Tuesday? Sick or…" I thought a moment for a good reason not to be here. I didn't have anywhere else to be. Then Mr. County Evaluator Man-hunk popped into my mind. Then I panicked. And out of my mouth came, "…or on a date?"

"Why on earth would you go on a date on a Tuesday morning, Ker?"

"You're missing the point. Point is—"

"I know, but she's so, so—"

"Insistent." The word boomed over the speakers and bounced around the customer-less store. Steve had left the glass office door open and could hear us below him at the registers. He still held the intercom's mic in his hand. He also didn't particularly enjoy the elderly Mrs. Halston's antics. And he wasn't wrong.

Insistent was the correct term for her.

By the time she killed her engine, Robby and Chris were coming across the lot from their spots under the oak trees. They saw her car, and Chris tried to retreat back to his pickup, but Rob grabbed him by the shirt and spun him forward. The boys, one high school and one high school dropout, approached Mrs. Halston's car, and, like good Midwestern gentleman, offered to help. Because, we all knew, the sooner we help, the sooner she'd be on her way.

Until the next Tuesday rolled around.

Savannah and I watch as the guys dutifully offer to hold her four-pronged walking cane as she maneuvers out of the car. I first see her black clunky slip-ons. Then the rim of her skirt. Today she wore the one with the sky-blue background and purple petunia print. Then I saw her head, only barely, poke up above her opened door as she stood all the way up. She may at one point have been five feet tall. But gravity and years shaved an inch or two off that. Her dark gray hair is always pulled up in a twisted bun and covered with a dainty black hair net.

Chris hands her the cane and she points it to the back seat where Rob retrieves an oversized reusable Save-N-Shop bag. Already full.

Steve moans into the intercom then killed the feed. He pulled from the window and focused down on whatever menial tasks await him at his desk. Savannah ducked behind the register to do her morning sanitation routine.

Rob walked a couple of steps behind Chris and Mrs. Halston. She'd knitted her shawl of beige yarn and it covered her shoulders and arms so just a couple of thin wrinkled hands peeked out. It hung all the way past her butt. Maybe she'd knitted it long ago when she was a few inches taller. Rob shook his head as he snuck one of the items out of the bag and held it up quickly behind their backs so I could see.

Another costume.

This time a pumpkin.

Deli Guy Gary was rounding the corner from the fresh meat case, likely to rib one of us with his dad jokes or tease with the nickname bit. Before he said a word, he took one look toward the door —where Chris was hopping up and down on the pressure plate to open the door and allow Mrs. Halston entrance. Gary spun on his heel and retreated into the depths of the store.

Well, there are small blessings…

"Good morning, Mrs. Halston. How are you today?"

"Fine Kerry. Just fine. A little nippy out." She hugged her shawl closer and motioned for Rob to hand me the shopping bag. "Time to switchem' out, dear." She smushed that word together. She'd made her own vocabulary for her craft.

The bag was heavier than last time. She'd been very busy.

"Well, let's get to it, shall we?" I really did have several tasks to attend to that had nothing to do with redressing thirty-five—well thirty-four now since Tall Dark Evaluator purchased one the other day—knitted unicorns.

Wait.

A handsome man like that.

Buying a prissy unicorn doll?

Why hadn't I thought of it?

You idiot. Kerry. You Freckle-Kinned idiot. He's got a kid.

All these days and weeks swooning and daydreaming and the man's got a daughter.

"You quite alright, Kerry?" Mrs. Halston had taken me by the arm and nudged me a little.

I tried to shake off the embarrassment, and though it was completely internal since no one knew what I'd been thinking and hoping for, it still stung like a swarm of wasps. "Yes, Mrs. Halston. I'm fine. I just remembered something, that's all."

"Oh, girl. That happens to me all the time. Always getting interrupted by something I don't want to think of. Maybe this little project of ours will help brighten your countenance."

I couldn't imagine any universe, no matter how dark my countenance, in which undressing knitted unicorn dolls from patriotic tutus and star-studded scarves of summer and redressing them with pumpkins and witch hats would brighten my countenance.

But the sooner we helped—I, the sooner I helped, as my cowardly coworkers wouldn't stoop so low as to pacify Mrs. Halston's obsession—the sooner she fills her reusable shopping bag with bread and milk and moves on with her day. Then we can move on with ours.

We go to the back corner of the store, and, as always, I point out the few loose tiles along the way. She's spry enough to remember but she politely thanks me each time. The last thing we need is a broken hip lawsuit from the unicorn lady.

Save-N-Shop has a tiny selection of live plants that we cosign for the local greenhouse, and I usually inflate a few birthday balloons and tie them to the display. We have one rack of greeting cards, most of them needed dusting.

And then, before you round the corner for the cereal aisle, tucked in the corner by the plants, is our largest non-food corner shelf display. I think it was meant to hold apples and oranges and such, but ever since I started here, it's held Mrs. Halston's knitted unicorns.

Only when I started here, they were all naked. Some were white bodied and some purple. Lots of yellow horns, though a few had black or blue ones with tiny specks of silver or gold knitted through. They were just the right size for a small child to tuck under their armpit and take on an adventure. And when I was four or five years old, I'd have loved one of these—naked or costumed, it wouldn't have mattered.

But, lately, I've had my fill of knitted unicorns.

Mrs. Halston and I began the process of undressing the steeds and mares from their summer attire. I pulled an identical empty Save-N-Shop reusable bag from under the unicorn display (I've learned a few tricks along the way to save time) and we tossed the red, white and blues into it as we went. Mrs. Halston rattled on as we worked about the same old stories. How they met. Their kids. How much she missed her family. I nod appropriately and try to not think about Mr. Evaluator Guy.

Steve and Mr. Halston—may he rest in peace—thought this project would give Mrs. Halston some closure after losing her family. Some to sickness, some to age. Some to just hard living. No one quite knew why she got hung up on horned horses, but that was beside the point. She needed an outlet for her craft, and Steve allowed her this corner.

And within a month, she'd filled the shelving unit with thirty-five knitted unicorns. "Priced to sell, priced to sell." But not one soul in Covort County cared about unicorns nearly as much as Mrs. Halston.

Then she took to making them costumes. "Added value, is what the marketing people call it. Added value." She wasn't wrong, but still, no nibbles.

Until Mr. Evaluator Guy.

"Oh, my good lord in heaven above." Mrs. Halston's gasp drew my full attention. Health concerns always concern me. Maybe because I wanted to go into nursing. Maybe because she's old and Save-N-Shop can't go under or I'd be uneducated and unemployed.

"What's wrong?" I dropped the glittery tutu into the sack and wrapped my arm around her frail shoulders. She didn't answer me but stared straight ahead at the shelf. "Mrs. Halston?"

"Kerry! You should've told me!"

"Oh. Yeah. That. An out-of-towner bought one the other day."

Her blue eyes filled with tears that she didn't bother holding back. She turned and buried her head in my smock and sobbed. "I knew it. I knew it. I knew if I waited long enough, someone else would appreciate them." She pulled back and dabbed her face with the shawl. My apron top was wet, but I didn't care. I was still worried the old gal might stroke out.

"Tell me, tell me about who bought it."

"Well, ma'am, I did."

I let go of Mrs. Halston and spun to see him. Mr. Evaluator guy. Standing behind me. All fatherly-like and polite with those crisp blue eyes. And he smelled so much better than the fresh roses the greenhouse gal brought yesterday. Startled, I took a slightly-too-wide of a step backward.

Into the herd of unicorns.

And the corner shelf which held up thirty-five—no thirty-four—knitted dolls broke under my weight. I was barely aware of controlling my legs, but my nurse-wannabe-brain was, and I managed to kick over a half-full sack of summer unicorn outfits and an entire sack-full of fall wardrobe bits and sent them everywhere.

Gary heard the ruckus and came running. Chris and Rob showed up next.

It all happened so fast.

And in front of THE GUY. Who reached for my hand while

Rob looked after a very startled Mrs. Halston and Gary helped THE GUY set me right again.

"Well, then, Freckle-Kinned Kerry. How 'bout that?" Not even a dad joke to soften the humiliation.

"Are you okay, Kerry?"

"Yeah. Well…" My face was redder than the stripes on our flag, I knew because I could feel the blood boiling under my cheeks. I tried to straighten myself up. My ponytail came loose and my hair was all a mess around my shoulders and hung in the way as I bent to try to save the unicorns from the rubble before Mrs. Halston had a cow—Wait.

Mrs. Halston. *Oh, my lord. I killed her mental health outlet.*

But she wasn't stroking out. She was belly laughing. So much so that she had to lean on her four-pronged walker and Rob at the same time.

Steve brought us a shopping cart. The gang, even Savannah, all helped free the unicorns from the rubble. Search and rescue, Save-N-Shop style, all while Mrs. Halston caught her breath.

"So, young man. Who was the recipient?" I froze mid-bend and looked up at her. She winked at me.

"Oh, my niece. She's a patient at St. Venue. Doing much better. But she loved her unicorn with the sparkling tutu. Just loved it."

"Niece, huh?" She winked at me. AGAIN. "Got any daughters that would like one as well?" Always the saleswoman. Always. I was mortified, heart pounding in my ears and as the adrenaline came and went in oceanic waves, I was starting to feel the effects of my fall. Ankle. Hip. Shoulder.

But mostly I just felt mortified. I let my hair hang in my face and kept cleaning up as I waited for his answer. By this time, a few customers, god bless their hearts, had gathered at the back corner and watched as their dear Save-N-Shop staff cleaned up the most magical of messes.

"So, your name, my dear first customer?" Someone handed Mrs. Halston a naked unicorn for her to dress as a pumpkin.

"Brian, ma'am. Brian Rogers."

She winked at me again. "He said 'ma'am.' And your niece's name?"

"Emily."

"How did little miss Emily like her gift?"

He tossed two more bodies into the cart. I fished out several scarves and a ripped tutu. "She loved it. Was the envy of the whole girls' wing." He paused and held one of the unicorns, turning it over in his hands. "You know, Mrs. Halston?"

Her eyes sparkled as if she knew what was coming.

"I think, I think…" Then he winked at me. Mr. Brian Rogers, the Evaluator Guy. My heart couldn't hand this kind of emotional whiplash. "I think I'll take the whole cart."

"All of them?" I choked. Whatever will we do on Tuesday mornings now?

"All the knitted unicorns. And their pretty little outfits, too. It'll do the hospital good to have them to pass out to the little girls."

Mrs. Halston clasped her hands together and nearly floated off the broken tile floor in her black flat slip-ons. "Oh, Brian. Oh, oh. Thank you soooo much."

We finished fishing out the thirty-four bodies, saved what summer and fall attire we could, and tossed everything into the cart. Steve insisted he pay Mrs. Halston directly, saved him the commission paperwork later.

We reached the parking lot amid the applause and bows of the ever-growing crowd, mostly that was for Mrs. Halston. I got a few well-earned happy heckles as the word spread on who broke the display. A couple of the younger, more tech-abled bodies likely live-streamed us. I probably already have memes.

"Got any nephews, Mr. Brian Rogers?"

"No, ma'am, why?" He shuffled the bags of costumes from the cart into the back of his rental car. I leaned against his shopping cart full of all the knitted unicorns and tried to decide what just happened.

She fished out her car keys from her shawl pocket and popped the trunk of her Buick.

"I've got thirty-five knitted red-winged dragons just waiting for good homes."

Brian's eyes widened. "No ma'am. No nephews."

"Well, maybe someday you'll have a little boy of your own, and you'll know just where to find him a dragon."

She winked at me again.

I know what I'll be doing next Tuesday morning.

About the Author

Beth enjoys chucking words into sentences then standing back to see what magic—or mayhem—falls out, crafting tales in mystery, sci-fi, fantasy, and general "slice of life" fiction. She couldn't accomplish this without the help of her tutu-clad Little Miss Muse and Trudi the Concrete Office Goose, who's partial to superhero capes.

Her stories have appeared in multiple publications, including Pulphouse Fiction Magazine and Ellery Queen Mystery Magazine, and in multiple fiction anthologies. She's received several Honorable Mentions from Writers of the Future. Her lighthearted blog peeks into the writing life as she pokes fun at herself and her circus of a life.

Follow the antics of Little Miss Muse and Trudi, read Beth's blog (she might have burned down her kitchen last week), and discover the stories at bapaul.com.

Also by B. A. Paul

Short Story Collections:

Spunk and Spice, Volumes 1 and 2: A Collection of six short stories celebrating timeless wit and wisdom.

Out There, Volumes 1 and 2: A Collection of six short sci-fi and speculative tales.

Mystery Minutes, Volumes 1 and 2: Six short mystery stories

All the Feels, Volumes 1, 2, and 3: Collections of inspiring short stories

Just a Tick of Whimsy, Volumes 1 and 2: Collections of fantasy shorts.

Hijacked Holidays: Definitely not your warm-and-fuzzy winter tales.

Dark Minds: Toe-curling twisted mysteries.

Blog Compilations: Slices of the writing life with lots of laughs and bumps in the road.

Life Along the Way

Life All Over Again

Novels

Triage

Young Adult (or Young at Heart)

Switch: Book 1 in the Oliver Andrews Trilogy

Keep In Touch!

BAPAUL.COM

Take a glimpse into B.A. Paul's writing journey, including the ups and downs of managing family, "real jobs," ducks in wobbling rows, and chasing down her Little Miss Muse. New blog posts go up Mondays, with the first Monday of the month reserved for a free fiction short story available on the blog for a limited time.

Newsletter Signup!

Get the latest release information, author updates, and exclusive content by signing up at bapaul.com.

www.ingramcontent.com/pod-product-compliance
Lightning Source LLC
Chambersburg PA
CBHW070355310726
48977CB00002B/454